It would only take one slip to end the campaign right here

Bolan made his decision and took the second frag grenade—his last—from his belt. Before he pulled the pin, he fired another short burst from the SMG to drill the truck's fuel tank, and rivulets of amber liquid began to trickle to the ground. He palmed the grenade, freed the pin, and made the long pitch overhand.

Three seconds later he was rewarded with a smoky thunderclap. Flames spread rapidly on trails of dribbling fuel until the truck's gas tank blew, the secondary blast engulfing half a dozen Serbs in swirling smoke and fire. One of the soldiers tried to escape from his hiding place beneath the truck, his hair and clothes in flames, but he was pinned, and his frantic screams added new confusion to the scene.

Survivors from the blast began to run for their lives. Bolan milked short bursts from his SMG, reloading swiftly when his magazine cycled dry, picking up one final runner almost at the limit of his range.

And that left two—one man wi[illegible] AK-47 and the other with a pistol.

MACK BOLAN®

The Executioner

#152 Combat Stretch
#153 Firebase Florida
#154 Night Hit
#155 Hawaiian Heat
#156 Phantom Force
#157 Cayman Strike
#158 Firing Line
#159 Steel and Flame
#160 Storm Warning
#161 Eye of the Storm
#162 Colors of Hell
#163 Warrior's Edge
#164 Death Trail
#165 Fire Sweep
#166 Assassin's Creed
#167 Double Action
#168 Blood Price
#169 White Heat
#170 Baja Blitz
#171 Deadly Force
#172 Fast Strike
#173 Capitol Hit
#174 Battle Plan
#175 Battle Ground
#176 Ransom Run
#177 Evil Code
#178 Black Hand
#179 War Hammer
#180 Force Down
#181 Shifting Target
#182 Lethal Agent
#183 Clean Sweep
#184 Death Warrant
#185 Sudden Fury
#186 Fire Burst
#187 Cleansing Flame
#188 War Paint
#189 Wellfire
#190 Killing Range
#191 Extreme Force
#192 Maximum Impact
#193 Hostile Action
#194 Deadly Contest
#195 Select Fire
#196 Triburst
#197 Armed Force
#198 Shoot Down
#199 Rogue Agent
#200 Crisis Point
#201 Prime Target
#202 Combat Zone
#203 Hard Contact
#204 Rescue Run
#205 Hell Road
#206 Hunting Cry

DON PENDLETON'S

THE EXECUTIONER®

HUNTING CRY

A GOLD EAGLE BOOK FROM
WORLDWIDE®

TORONTO • NEW YORK • LONDON
AMSTERDAM • PARIS • SYDNEY • HAMBURG
STOCKHOLM • ATHENS • TOKYO • MILAN
MADRID • WARSAW • BUDAPEST • AUCKLAND

First edition February 1996
ISBN 0-373-64206-7

Special thanks and acknowledgment to
Mike Newton for his contribution to this work.

HUNTING CRY

Printed in U.S.A.

As soon as the people fix up one Shame of the World, another turns up.

—Edgar Watson Howe

The shame of human bondage has been masked by silence long enough. It's time to let some righteous rage take hold and light a cleansing fire. Anyone who gets in the way can expect to get burned.

—Mack Bolan

To the members of the United Nations peacekeeping forces who served in Bosnia-Herzegovina.

PROLOGUE

The shelling stopped at dawn. Concealed within her basement shelter, Vasvija Validmic thought about the gunners she'd never seen, and waited for the rapid-fire explosions to resume. It took nearly an hour for her to decide that this wasn't a simple respite for the Serbs, but something more.

Ironically she found the sudden, eerie silence more unnerving than the shelling that had scourged Bugojno for the past three days.

Vasvija knew about surviving in a war zone. Eight months earlier at the age of nineteen, she'd been orphaned, her parents killed by mortar fire. The searchers had found them lying side by side beneath a ton of rubble, hands outstretched and almost touching, as if they'd somehow tried to renew their wedding vows in death.

Vasvija's brother, Haris, was the next to die, cut down by snipers on the outskirts of Bugojno. His death had been neither quick nor clean. The bullet had drilled his liver, and he'd spent five hours gasping out his life in a field hospital that had once been an elementary school.

There was no place for education these days in Bugojno. Normal childhood was a fading memory, a fairy tale to those born after independence and the outbreak of her country's ethnic civil war.

Her country?

It was true that Muslims like Vasvija made up a forty-three percent majority in the young country of Bosnia-Herzegovina, but numbers meant little. The Serbs constituted less than one-third of the population, yet their superior stockpile of weapons, combined with their driving hatred for the Muslims, had given them a crucial edge in the war.

Bugojno had been lucky for a while. Located fifty miles northwest of Sarajevo, it had managed to escape the worst of "ethnic cleansing" in the early stages, when mortal combat was centered around the capital. But in the spring of 1994, sporadic mortar rounds and rockets began to give way to systematic sniper fire and shelling that amounted to a full-scale siege. Twice the major roads were cut, and supplies had to be airlifted from the capital until the land routes were restored. Despite a UN arms embargo favoring the Serbs, Muslim militiamen held the line against infiltrators and guerrilla raiding parties, giving nearly as good as they got on a small-unit, one-to-one basis.

They couldn't match the heavy artillery, though. Shells bombarded Bugojno day and night, turning the once-peaceful streets into a cratered moonscape, and leaving shops and houses shattered. Normal life had shuddered to a halt, daily routines transformed into a living hell of fire brigades and burial parties, makeshift first-aid stations and people scavenging the streets for food.

It had been four days since she'd last seen Janez, her fiancé, on his way to fight with the militia north of the town. For all Vasvija knew he might be dead, and while the thought was painful to her, it carried with it little of the overwhelming grief she would have expected. There was so much death around her that her heart and mind had almost grown numb.

It was approaching half-past seven when she heard the first reports of small-arms fire echoing from several blocks away. Her basement hideout lay five hundred yards behind the line of battle, but she felt a sudden urge to flee, to find somewhere else to hide. Artillery was one thing, but the troops who came on foot could find her.

And Vasvija knew about the special punishment reserved for Muslim women by the Serbs.

Her heart was pounding as she scrambled from the basement, through a window long since cleared of glass by an explosion in the street. Her hands and face were smudged with soot, her clothing soiled and torn. But Vasvija knew that compared to many of her neighbors, she was fortunate.

She was still alive.

But for how long?

And if the Serbs should catch her, would she wish to live?

The battle sounds came from the north, so Vasvija ran southward, putting another hundred yards behind her without meeting another survivor. There were bodies in the street, unburied since the last barrage had torn through Bugojno, but she didn't stop to see if any of her friends or neighbors were among them.

She had to find another place to hide.

She avoided a pharmacy and a grocery store, knowing both would rate attention from the Serbs if they broke through and started looting. It was better to select a place that held no interest for them, offered nothing for them to steal.

Vasvija chose a candlemaker's shop that had survived a near miss from artillery, with two walls and a portion of the roof intact. Inside, a pall of dust and smoke hung over everything, and great pools of colored candle wax had melted on the floor like giant bloodstains. It made for slippery footing, but she did her best to skirt the worst parts, wishing she had some way to erase the tracks she left behind in the wax.

She would pray to God that the infidels were stopped before they got this far—and, failing that, for them to miss her when they searched the street.

Vasvija felt the warm tears on her cheeks before she realized she was weeping. It was plainly fear this time, instead of grief or loss that made her tremble in the shadows. She had listened to the tales of refugees, survivors from Jelec, Rizvanovici, Brcko and a dozen other Muslim settlements in Bosnia. She knew about the hundreds of kidnappings, rapes and other sexual atrocities inflicted on the girls and women of her faith.

While rape, to some extent, had always been a brutal side effect of war, in Bosnia-Herzegovina it was now a formal strategy among her enemies. The Serbs knew well enough how Muslims valued chastity, the shame that followed intercourse outside of wedlock, even when the female was brutalized against her will. Virginity—at least for women—was a firm prerequisite for marriage, and where pregnancy resulted from a rape, the mother and her child alike were treated as outcasts, driven from their home and family in everlasting shame.

Vasvija became aware of the oppressive silence only by degrees. When had the small-arms firing ceased?

It seemed impossible that the militiamen had managed to repel the Serbs. How could they, when the kindest estimates had them outnumbered five or six to one? It seemed more likely that the last of them had finally been killed or captured by the enemy, to leave Bugojno finally defenseless.

Leaving *her* defenseless.

Panic drove Vasvija from her hiding place out to the rubble-strewn sidewalk. She stared up the street, just in time to see an armored personnel carrier turn a corner three blocks away, with troops in camouflage fatigues fanned out around the vehicle. Their eyes and rifles swept the empty street.

She recognized the men as Serbs.

Too late she scuttled back inside the candlemaker's shop and tucked herself behind the burned-out hulk of a display case. She heard the armored vehicle approaching, then harsh male voices calling back and forth. Boot heels crunched on broken glass as they moved from the street into the shop. She held her breath, as much to quell the brisk, erratic throbbing of her heart as to prevent the scouts from hearing her and following the sound to where she lay.

It didn't help.

The footsteps drew closer, pausing just beyond the far side of the ruined showcase. Huddled on the floor, Vasvija felt as if her lungs were bursting. She tried to turn her head to look up without producing any sound.

A dark face swam into her field of vision.

"What have we here?" The voice was mocking.

"A little bird." The new voice came from somewhere to her right. "We should pluck it, don't you think?"

"In time. We have our orders at the moment."

"The major doesn't mind if we amuse ourselves," the disembodied voice came back. "In fact we have his blessing."

"Only when the prizes are collected," the first man said, circling around the showcase to approach Vasvija.

She tried to jerk away from him, and a second pair of hands moved in to drag her upright. She was trapped between the two Serbs as they brought her to her feet and forced her back against the nearest standing wall.

Both men were armed with automatic rifles. Vasvija knew little of such things, but they appeared to be what her fiancé called Kalashnikovs. It occurred to her that she should make a grab for one of the rifles, at least attempt to save herself. No matter that she didn't know the first thing about cocking, aiming or firing such a weapon. If they killed her on the spot, she would be spared the defilement that waited for her in captivity.

But her courage failed her, and she could offer no resistance when one soldier began to fondle her. He squeezed her breast and was about to thrust his hand between her trembling legs when his companion stopped him with a snarl.

"Not yet, I told you! We must take her back to camp."

The soldier reluctantly took his hand away, but he leaned close to whisper in Vasvija's ear, "Tonight, I'll have you."

Her legs could scarcely hold her upright as they led her from the shop and out to the street. They prodded her with rifles, cursing when she stumbled, while the soldier continued to keep up a steady stream of comments about the things he intended to do with her when he got the chance.

Outside, she found at least a dozen soldiers ringed around the shop front, waiting for their comrades to emerge. The armored vehicle stood close behind them, its engine idling, its twin machine guns pointed at the shop. At her.

A military truck with a canvas top drew to halt in front of the shop, its tires crunching rubble in the street. Vasvija's captors shoved her rudely toward the back of the vehicle. One of them offered his hand to help her up. She spurned it, but he used the opportunity to grab her buttocks before she tottered out of reach.

Another soldier sat in the truck, his rifle covering three women seated on a wooden bench opposite him. Vasvija took her place as fourth in line, making sure that her tattered skirt covered her knees. She kept her eyes down mostly, shooting little glances at her fellow captives, picking out their cuts and bruises, and the rips in their clothing.

The hostage closest to her was a teenage girl, no more than seventeen years old, who clutched herself with folded arms and wept incessantly. The buttons of her yellow blouse were gone, a few threads dangling where they'd been ripped away, and she'd tried to wrap the bright material around her to hide her breasts. The way she sobbed and trembled, Vasvija reckoned that the girl had suffered more than a fondling by her captors.

They made slow progress—one block at a time—with frequent stops as members of the infantry patrol checked shops and houses for potential loot or prisoners. Four more women were collected in the next two hours, and another soldier was placed inside the truck to help his comrade guard them.

Vasvija had no wristwatch, but she was fairly certain that they spent at least four hours prowling through Bugojno's streets, collecting prisoners—all female—in the canvas-covered truck. From time to time, when men or boys were found, she heard staccato bursts of gunfire, and then the vehicles moved on. At other points, when they were stopped for any reason, soldiers from the ground team lingered near the tailgate of the truck and eyed the female prisoners as if they were cuts of beef displayed in a butcher's window.

Finally, when Vasvija had grown numb from sitting on the wooden bench, they completed their tour and put Bugojno behind them. They had only searched a portion of the town, but once they cleared the outskirts, she saw other trucks and armored vehicles behind them. Vasvija realized there had to have been several patrols dispatched to cover the town.

It took nearly another hour and a half to reach their final destination. Barbed-wire fencing was her first glimpse of the camp once they'd passed through the gate, with armed guards covering the motorcade. The truck stopped short a moment later, and the guards unloaded, barking orders at their captives to do likewise.

It was difficult to walk at first, on legs that ached and tingled. Vasvija came close to falling as she left the truck, but caught herself before the soldiers could step in with their groping hands.

Along with her fellow prisoners, Vasvija was directed to a sort of barracks, where a further two dozen captives waited, perched either on folding cots or standing near the fly-speckled windows. There was no apparent uniform for the inmates of the camp, although several wore baggy, shapeless dresses cut from faded material, identical in all but color. Everywhere she looked, Vasvija saw the same dazed, haunted expression in the eyes of the women.

She found a vacant cot, stripped of bedding, and sat, her shoulders braced against the wall, her knees drawn up close against her chest and circled with her arms. She'd stopped trembling now, although dread still sat upon her shoulder like a raven.

Vasvija didn't listen when some of the women started to whisper among themselves. She tried to close her ears, and when that failed, began to hum low in her throat to drown out the voices.

The afternoon was fading into purple dusk when they returned, five ragged-looking soldiers with rifles slung over their shoulders. Vasvija refused to face them as they moved between the rows of cots, but they didn't ignore her. Two of them stopped at her cot, one soldier reaching down and pulling her up roughly when she refused to stand.

Vasvija struggled briefly, until one of them balled his fist and struck her on the head with enough force to stun her. She was barely conscious as the rest of the soldiers seized the teenage girl who'd ridden beside her in the truck.

When they dragged Vasvija outside, a cool breeze blew the hair across her face. The evening sky looked bruised.

It was a quarter-hour later when the women still inside the barracks heard Vasvija start to scream.

1

"It's close," Zeljko Maksimovic said, his hands white-knuckled on the steering wheel.

Seated beside him, Mack Bolan, a.k.a. the Executioner, glanced at his wristwatch to confirm that it was nearly 2:00 a.m. The road in front of them was dark, and they were driving without lights for security reasons. There was nothing Bolan could do about the engine noise, but he trusted that his enemies would mostly be asleep by now. Or maybe they'd be wide awake and waiting for him.

Either way, the Executioner intended to proceed.

The target was a boarding school located on the outskirts of Zvornik, five miles inland from the Adriatic coast of Bosnia. The school had been shut down when civil war erupted in that portion of the former Yugoslavia. Serb insurrectionists now controlled the complex and had converted it to a military prison. With a difference.

According to the information Bolan had been given, all the prisoners inside the Zvornik camp were female noncombatants, held as "entertainment" for the Serbs.

In other words, it was a military brothel, using prisoners in place of prostitutes.

Maksimovic, Bolan's driver, was a Muslim, short and wiry, with a cloth cap covering his unkempt, curly hair. His pants and jacket were denim, and his dark shirt was open at the collar. A Czech-made Skorpion machine pistol lay on the bench seat, close against his thigh.

Bolan wore a combat blacksuit under military webbing. A Desert Eagle .44 Magnum automatic rode his right hip in fast-draw leather, while the select-fire Beretta 93-R was secure in a shoulder leather beneath his left armpit. His lead weapon was a Heckler & Koch MP-5 SD-3 submachine gun, complete with telescoping stock and a factory-standard suppressor. Spare magazines for his weapons were slotted into pouches at his waist and on the bandoleer across his chest.

None of the three weapons—Italian, German and Israeli—was traceable to Bolan or the States if one or more of them were somehow lost on the battleground.

"One more minute," Maksimovic said.

The Executioner was ready, running through the compound's blueprint in his mind, confirming his original impression that he'd selected the best angle of attack. His sources estimated that there were ten or fifteen watchdogs guarding the complex at any given time, plus an unknown number of the enemy that might be sleeping over, with their weapons close at hand.

Ahead, Bolan saw the squarish bulk of the institution looming against the night. Four hours remained before the dawn arrived to help his enemies. Meanwhile, he had the darkness, motivation and the palpable advantage of surprise.

The final hundred yards was downhill, a gentle slope that leveled off exactly where the school had been constructed, at the intersection of a two-lane highway and a smaller access road that ran across the route of their approach. Maksimovic killed the engine as he topped the rise and took the old truck out of gear. A combination of gravity and momentum did the rest, taking them downhill at a steady clip.

He braked at the bottom of the slope, slowing enough for Bolan to bail out.

It was supposed to be a relatively simple in-and-out operation, but Bolan knew that things were rarely simple in the hellgrounds.

He let the darkness cover him as he approached the complex. No outer sentry challenged him. Was that complacency, a feeling that the Muslims had no stomach for resisting tyranny, or was there something he'd missed?

If it turned out to be the latter, he'd know it soon enough.

Meanwhile, a good offense wasn't only the best defense. From Bolan's point of view, it was the only game in town.

CAPTAIN RADOVAN BASSIOUNI woke from a fitful sleep and wondered what had roused him. Still wearing the bottom half of his uniform, he lay still atop his rumpled bed, listening for any new, suspicious sounds while last night's vodka made its presence felt.

The Zvornik brothel post was weak on military protocol. Bassiouni still required his men to call him "Sir" and go through the motions of saluting him, but he had little energy for tedious administrative duties and none at all for rigorous inspections and the like.

The war was being fought by others—Captain Bassiouni's problems were of a different sort. From time to time, one of the captives tried to run away, but it was rare; their spirits had been broken for the most part, as intended, and they had nowhere to go. More commonly there would be trouble from the soldiers, quarrels inflamed by lust, jealousy and vodka. Field commanders hated it when troops were injured on a furlough, and it was Bassiouni's ultimate responsibility to see that no harm befell the troops before they could be slaughtered on the battlefield.

There had been half a dozen deaths at Zvornik, but the casualties had all been Muslim women, killed by overzealous lovers. Bassiouni took no action in such cases, other than requesting fresh replacements. Killing Muslims was the point of ethnic cleansing after all, and each dead woman was one less to perpetuate the breed.

Bassiouni had just begun to think that perhaps a dream had shaken him awake, when suddenly he heard a muffled shout, immediately followed by a burst of automatic weapons' fire. Bassiouni's first thought was that the sounds were coming from the small gymnasium where he confined the prisoners when they weren't engaged with the soldiers in one or another of the school's dozen classrooms.

Lurching to his feet, he grabbed his balled-up shirt from a nearby chair and tried to put it on, but it defeated him, and in a fit of fury he abandoned the attempt and flung the garment down. He stumbled across to the cheap vanity table where his pistol belt lay coiled. He got the buckle fastened on his third attempt and drew the Makarov 9 mm pistol from its holster, flicking off the safety as he moved toward the door.

Bassiouni's quarters had once been the headmaster's office, a selection he found appropriate in terms of his rank and position in the prison compound. Stepping from the door, he faced an open courtyard with classrooms on three sides and the gymnasium directly opposite his door. The courtyard had four exits, open breezeways at each corner, corresponding with the major compass points. The only lighting was a floodlight mounted directly over the gymnasium's double doors, where one guard was habitually stationed by day, two after nightfall.

Bassiouni saw that both men were missing from their post and that the left-hand door was ajar. Beyond the threshold all was darkness, but both male and female voices could be heard crying out as automatic weapons went off like muffled fireworks.

Bassiouni started to shout for his troops and fired two shots skyward in his urgency to gather reinforcements. That left six rounds in the magazine, with two spare clips on his belt. But the captain didn't plan on dueling with his adversaries personally. He had thirteen soldiers on the grounds for such contingencies, although it had never seriously crossed his mind to plan for an assault.

As troops began to respond to the sounds of shouts and gunfire, Bassiouni moved cautiously toward the gymnasium, waving his soldiers before him. The gunfire from the gym seemed to have stopped. Had the guards eliminated the invaders, or had his men been killed?

The women had fallen silent now as well, and that disturbed Bassiouni more than anything. There hadn't been sufficient fire, in is view, to wipe out twenty women. Silence to him meant that they were either frightened, or...

The other possibility made Bassiouni shout fresh orders at the soldiers, demanding that they hurry, penetrate the gym and find out what was happening. He was sweating, even though the night breeze was cool against his bare chest.

The rest of Bassiouni's men had joined him, some with their shirts unbuttoned, one or two even barefoot, but all armed. The ones who had been asleep looked confused and disoriented.

"Get after them!" the captain shouted. "Hurry up, you slackers!"

First one man and then another reached the threshold of the open door and peered into the darkness, hesitating for a beat before stepping inside. Bassiouni held his breath and waited, listening for voices, gunshots, anything. It seemed to take forever. Then he heard the stutter of Kalashnikovs, two weapons hammering as one.

"Go on!" he ordered the remaining troops. "They need you! Hurry!"

As they moved forward, Bassiouni gave them ample room. Only then did he follow, stepping gingerly into the dark gymnasium.

THE WAITING TROUBLED Zeljko Maksimovic. Seated in the truck with both windows down and the engine idling quietly, he tried to guess what had to be happening inside. The women weren't known to him, but they were of his faith. Maksimovic had known that this was a special case from the moment the Americans had become involved. More than two years had passed since newsmen from around the world had first documented widespread, systematic rape of Muslim women by the Serbs in Bosnia. Aside from diplomatic protests and hot air in the United Nations, nothing had been done, until the word came down that an American was on his way to help.

Maksimovic wasn't entirely clear on what had sparked the sudden interest, and he knew one man could do only so much. Still, it was something, and if Maksimovic had to risk his own life, he would do so gladly.

He'd coasted silently past the building and started the engine again when he was ten or fifteen yards beyond the complex. He'd then made a U-turn in the middle of the road and driven back to the southeast corner of the building, stopping behind the small gymnasium. His orders were to wait for the American, the man who had been introduced to him as Mike Belasko. Fifteen minutes was supposed to be the limit, but Maksimovic knew he wouldn't leave without his passengers unless he had some concrete knowledge of their fate.

The Skorpion was heavy in his lap, his right hand sweating where it clutched the wooden pistol grip. His other hand gripped the steering wheel. His eyes were focused squarely on the closed back door of the gym from which the women and their savior would emerge—if they survived. But if Serbs erupted through the door, instead of Belasko and the women, Maksimovic would open fire on them and try to flee. Whatever happened, he wouldn't let the bastards capture him alive.

According to Maksimovic's watch, it had taken three minutes from the time Belasko had left the moving truck for chaotic sounds and voices to erupt from the gymnasium. Then the sound of automatic weapons had followed immediately. Belasko's submachine gun had a sound suppressor. What he heard was the telltale clatter of Kalashnikovs.

He raised the Skorpion, resting its muzzle on the windowsill, its sights fixed on the door. His index finger tightened on the trigger, taking up the slack, so that it would take only a twitch to spray the door and wall with 7.65 mm bullets.

Perspiration beaded on Maksimovic's brow and ran down his face. The shirt felt clammy on his back, and he could feel a nagging itch between his shoulder blades.

After about thirty seconds the gunfire stopped, and Maksimovic lost the sound of voices from within the building. Seconds later he heard what sounded like a pistol shot from beyond the gym. A warning, probably to rouse the guards.

They were swiftly running out of time.

He sat and waited, swallowing an urge to leave the truck and find out what was happening inside the gym. Any deviation from his orders could result in disaster. If sitting and waiting got him killed, so be it. He would do as he was told, but he wouldn't relax his guard.

If any of the enemy appeared, he would send them off to meet their eternal judgment.

THE FIRST GUARD Bolan met on his approach was a young man in camouflage fatigues. He raised his weapon, and Bolan let fly with his Ka-bar fighting knife. The soldier slid silently to the ground.

The Serb had been standing guard outside a locked metal door. The Executioner knelt and used a pick on the simple mechanism, feeling the tumblers click in seconds flat. He stood and with his finger on the MP-5 SD-3's trigger slipped across the threshold into the darkness.

For a moment it seemed absolutely silent, then his ears picked up the sound of voices whispering somewhere in front of him. He waited for his pupils to adjust to the darkness. A rank of folding bleachers was to his right, and to the left, some distance to one side, a cloying smell of urine warned him that the toilets had malfunctioned.

In front of him, the main gymnasium area, roughly two dozen figures huddled on the hardwood floor. No cots or creature comforts were evident from where he stood. The latest information had told him to expect a minimum of twenty women in the compound, maybe more. Bolan didn't bother with a head count, since he had no intention of leaving anyone behind.

He stepped into the open room, his long strides propelling him toward the group. By the time he reached them, several women had noticed him. They began to exchange breathless whispers. While he didn't understand their language, Bolan guessed that they mistook him for a guard who'd abandoned his post to prey on those he was assigned to watch.

Bolan had rehearsed a few stock phrases with Maksimovic to facilitate the operation, and he used them now, his voice low-pitched but loud enough for all those present to hear.

"I'm a friend," he told them. "An American. I've come to set you free. There is a truck outside. We have no time to waste."

Some of the women started talking all at once, the volume picking up.

"Quiet!" Bolan snapped, his voice like tempered steel. "I only speak a little of your language, but I need your trust. Please hurry."

Half of the women had scrambled to their feet before he'd finished speaking, leaving rumpled blankets where they fell.

Bolan never knew exactly what it was that brought the sentries in before he had a chance to move the women in the direction of the exit.

"Get down!" he ordered as he moved out to meet the threat.

Two soldiers barged in, backlit by the floodlights from outside. Bolan fired a short burst at the leading silhouette. It was low, and he saw the gunner drop, his legs shattered, his voice raised in a cry of pain and outrage. Close behind him, the second soldier cut loose with a Kalashnikov, but his aim was spoiled as his companion fell against him. The initial rounds went high and wide, and glass rained from the fluorescent fixtures overhead.

Bolan crouched, returning fire with greater accuracy, nailing both guards with a figure eight that finished off the wounded Serb and dropped his partner into a boneless sprawl. He watched the open doorway for another moment, half expecting more troops to appear, but all seemed quiet.

It was now or never.

"Quickly! To the door!"

A pistol shot came from outside, but Bolan ignored it. He knew it was inevitable that his clash with the two sentries would alert the camp. It was a race now, with the odds against survival.

The women didn't seem to doubt him now, or if they did, the circumstances made them keep it to themselves. They rushed the door in haste, but not in panic, lining up to clear the threshold in a way that reminded him of the residents of any prison he'd ever seen. He didn't need a master's degree in psychology to know these women had been through the mill. They were beaten, maybe broken, but they still had strength enough to make one final bid for freedom.

Bolan hoped that, having come this far, he wouldn't let them down.

The truck was right on time, and Maksimovic left the cab at the sight of Bolan's company. He left the engine running, ran around to the back to drop the tailgate and assist the women to board. The Executioner, meanwhile, took a rear-guard post, prepared for anything.

Four women still had to board the truck when five soldiers came through the double doors, crouching, dodging, barking questions back and forth as their weapons scanned for a target.

Bolan took out the one in the front, slamming a burst of parabellum shockers through his chest, and pivoted to find another mark before the first man had even fallen. His second target was retreating toward the nearest bank of bleachers when a 3-round burst went home between his shoulder blades and dropped him.

The other soldiers were laying down a screen of fire with AK-47s as the Executioner ducked out and slammed the metal door of the truck behind him. There was no way to secure it, but speed mattered most right now. He flung himself across the tailgate of the truck and crouched among the women as Maksimovic stepped on the accelerator.

The only question left in Bolan's mind was whether they could travel far and fast enough to save themselves.

2

The last thing Captain Radovan Bassiouni had expected when he went to bed that night was any kind of mass escape, several of his soldiers dead and a car chase through the darkness. But now, he found himself hunched in the front seat of a staff car, with soldiers packed into the seat behind him. Others followed closely behind in a truck whose headlights blazed into the car's rearview mirror.

Bassiouni gripped the Makarov in his hand, as much to keep himself steady as from the hope he'd find a living target. He'd let his soldiers do the killing when it came to that, but he was forced by rank and circumstance to make a show of leadership.

And there was fear, as well. If Bassiouni allowed the women to escape, he'd be stripped of his command, perhaps demoted. It wasn't beyond the realm of possibility that charges would be filed. If dereliction of duty during wartime was alleged, and Bassiouni was convicted, he might well be shot.

One of his men had told Bassiouni that the women and their rescuers had escaped by truck. The lighter, faster staff car had an advantage, and suddenly Bassiouni caught a glimpse of brake lights up ahead as they approached a curve.

"Get after them!" Bassiouni shouted at his driver. "Hurry up!"

"Yes, sir."

The car surged forward, trailing dust behind it on the unpaved road, the ruts and potholes sending painful jolts along Bassiouni's spine. He cursed and braced his free hand on the dashboard, leaning forward as if he could force the vehicle on to even greater speed. Behind them the truck carrying nine more soldiers struggled to keep pace.

THE STEADILY GAINING headlights told Bolan he'd have to find a place in which to stand and fight. If they were overtaken on the so-called highway, and the truck damaged by gunfire, they could find themselves totally cut off, with no hope of escaping to the coast.

And that, in turn, would doom his larger mission.

The women, he reckoned, would be in for certain punishment—perhaps the lethal kind—no matter what became of him and Maksimovic. Common decency dictated that he do whatever possible to keep the women safe and help them elude their brutal captors.

And he only saw one way to go. He would have to stage an ambush.

Bolan rose from his crouched position in the back of the truck and moved between the frightened women toward the tailgate. He strung one leg across the tailgate, held on to the metal ribbing of the cover with his right hand and craned his neck to get a look at the darkened road ahead. There seemed to be another curve, perhaps two hundred yards ahead, where wooded slopes pressed close on either side. A glance back at their pursuers told him that they were trailing at least half a mile behind.

Bolan scrambled back across the tailgate, feeling the anxious eyes of the women upon him as he reached the window separating Maksimovic from the passengers. The sliding window opened at his touch, and Bolan spoke with urgency.

"Can you see that highway cut ahead, with trees on either side?"

"Yes."

"I'm getting off there. You don't have to stop, just slow enough to give me half a chance. Keep on for a thousand yards or so beyond the curve, then wait and see what happens. If my plan works out, you'll know it. If it doesn't, you'll still have a lead."

"I'd rather help you fight," Maksimovic said.

"There's no time for that," Bolan replied. "You're in charge of seeing that the women make it home. If I blow this, you'll get your chance to fight another time."

He reached through the opening, squeezed the young man's shoulder in a parting gesture and retreated once more to the tailgate. They had halved the distance to his drop point while they'd been speaking and Bolan new it was nearly time for him to make the jump.

He felt the truck begin to slow as Maksimovic downshifted carefully, avoiding the telltale flash of brake lights in the darkness. Bolan gave the young man credit for his thinking under pressure, hoping this wouldn't turn out to be the night Maksimovic learned how well he could function under hostile fire.

He heard a woman's startled cry as he left the truck, knew what she and her companions had to be thinking. Was the man who'd freed them from the compound deserting them? Were they once more alone against their enemies?

Bolan touched down on his feet, whipped through an agile shoulder roll and came up running to his left along the gentler slope, with the mingled evergreens and conifers providing hand and footholds as he climbed. They also granted added cover as he sought a vantage point from which to scourge his enemies.

He found it, less than halfway up the slope. He braced one heel against the nearest tree trunk, grinding with his hips until the soft earth shifted to accommodate his buttocks. Headlights bore down toward him through the darkness, below and to his left.

The range was average for Bolan's SMG, roughly fifty feet from his hideout to the middle of the narrow unpaved road. He unclipped a fragmentation grenade from his web belt, placed the SMG across his lap and pulled the grenade's safety pin. There was no turning back.

He marked his target with a mental X and gauged the distance. It should be an easy pitch if the few small saplings didn't get in the way. Before the egg touched down, his SMG would be on target, ready to unleash a stream of parabellum manglers even as the charge went off.

And Bolan hoped the double punch would be enough.

He had to stop his adversaries, block the road if possible and end the chase right here. His targets all had weapons, probably more powerful than Bolan's, and the soldiers who survived his ambush beyond the first ten seconds would be fighting back with everything they had.

There was no guarantee that he would walk away from this one. But then there never was. Each time he took a mission, Bolan's life was riding on the line.

And it would only take one slip to end the new campaign right here, right now.

IT SEEMED TO CAPTAIN Bassiouni that the truck they were pursuing slowed for just a moment entering a curve, but he couldn't be certain from such a distance, and no brake lights flared in the dark.

He scanned the roadway and both shoulders ahead of him. Trees pressed close on either side, and once they started through the curve, they'd be flanked by hillsides rising at an angle of approximately forty-five degrees. An army could be hidden there, Bassiouni realized, but it was difficult for him to imagine any Muslim force of consequence existing in the area.

The captain's palm was sweating as he gripped the Makarov. He switched hands with the pistol for a moment, wiped his clammy palm against his trouser leg, then took the weapon back in his right hand. He cocked the hammer with his thumb but kept the pistol pointed at the floorboard of the car, between his feet. The vehicle's top was down, which would give him ample room to raise the gun and fire when necessary.

"Faster!"

"Yes, sir."

They were closing in on the curve now, but the fleeing vehicle was nowhere in sight.. Then Bassiouni glimpsed a small, round object tumbling through the glare of the headlights. Thinking it might be a fir cone or some bit of windblown rubbish falling from the trees that overhung the roadway, he wasn't prepared for the explosion, the smoke and thunder and the singing shrapnel. The road heaved up in front of them, and he could feel the staff car swerving, becoming briefly airborne before going on its side, then sliding nosefirst into the left-hand shoulder of the road, where it finally jolted to a halt.

The seat belt that he'd fastened more by instinct than by conscious decision saved him. Somehow Bassiouni had held on to his pistol, his free arm raised to shield his face and head as they were swallowed by a roiling dust cloud. Seconds passed while he tried to regain his bearings. He felt something warm and wet spattering his face, and a deadweight pressed against his shoulder. He recognized the driver slumped against him, fresh blood streaming from a gash above his eye.

There was no response from the driver when Bassiouni tried to push him away. Whether he was unconscious or dead made no difference at the moment. The captain unbuckled his seat belt, wriggled free of his burden and worked his way out of the staff car. Its engine had stalled, and Bassiouni could smell oil as he struggled out an all fours.

Bassiouni glanced around for help and found one of his soldiers pinned beneath the staff car, obviously dead. Two others were alive and scrambling for the weapons they'd dropped when they were thrown clear of the vehicle.

The truck with Bassiouni's handful of support troops had swerved to a halt when the bomb detonated. Its engine had also stalled, and the driver was desperately trying to start it again but with no luck. His shotgun rider and the seven men in back were spraying automatic gunfire left and right, their bullets peppering the trees on both sides of the roadway.

Bassiouni couldn't tell if they had valid targets. The most important thing for him was to remove himself from any unseen adversary's line of fire.

As if in response to his thoughts, a line of bullets kicked up dust and grit a short yard to his left. Bassiouni flinched and scurried to conceal himself behind the overturned staff car. It was dark there, with the headlights shattered, and nothing but erratic muzzle-flashes illuminated the claustrophobic battleground.

How many Muslims were there in the ambush party? Did they have a chance? Could he somehow slip out on his own?

A bullet struck the staff car, ricocheted, and was immediately followed by another and yet another. There was no way for Bassiouni to compute the angle, and he didn't try. The very fact of death so near at hand came close to paralyzing him. It was so different from his training, years ago, or the reports of distant gunfire that would sometimes echo through the hills surrounding Zvornik as his people fought to crush the Muslim traitors.

This was life and death—*his* life or death.

How long before a bullet found him, and his blood was spattered on the field of combat?

Soon, unless he found a better place to hide.

Bassiouni turned and started crawling toward the trees.

THE SMG WASN'T IDEAL for potting targets crouched inside a military vehicle, but Bolan's enemies were frightened and disoriented, more intent on scrambling to save themselves than putting up an organized defense. They started off by spraying both sides of the road with automatic gunfire with no visible targets, and Bolan left them to it for a moment while the dust cleared, giving him a better field of fire.

The truck had stalled from all appearances, and Bolan canceled out the driver's hasty efforts to restart it with a short burst to the hood and right front tire. His aim was true, and he could plainly see the punctured tire as it went flat.

The first real hit on their vehicle galvanized the Serbs. They scattered, dodging to the left and right. Bolan counted at least six or seven of them before a couple quickly wriggled underneath the truck.

The soldiers below him began firing in all directions now, with some of their rounds coming dangerously close. Their strength was concentrated under and around the truck, with two or three guns firing from behind the capsized staff car.

Bolan made his decision and took the second frag grenade—his last one—from his belt. Before he pulled the pin, he fired another short burst from the SMG to drill the truck's fuel tank, and rivulets of amber liquid began to trickle to the ground. He palmed the grenade, freed the pin and made the long pitch overhand. Once it landed on the dirt and gravel road, the grenade began to roll, its wobbling progress visible until it vanished underneath the truck.

Three seconds later Bolan was rewarded with a smoky thunderclap. Flames spread rapidly on trails of dribbling fuel until the truck's gas tank blew, the secondary blast engulfing half a dozen Serbs in swirling smoke and fire. One of the soldiers tried to escape from his hiding place beneath the truck, his hair and clothes in flames, but he was pinned, and his screams added new confusion to the scene.

Survivors from the blast began to run for their lives. Bolan had his pick of moving targets, and he milked short bursts from his SMG. There was no resistance now, although the soldiers triggered frantic, aimless bursts with their weapons as they tried to flee. The Executioner dropped each of them in turn, reloading swiftly when his magazine cycled dry, picking up one final runner almost at the limit of his range.

And that left two behind the staff car—one man with an AK-47 and the other with a pistol. Neither was firing at the moment, but the rifleman kept popping up to look for targets, playing hide-and-seek with Bolan from a distance.

He could leave them as they were, immobilized, rejoin the women and Maksimovic, safe now from an immediate pursuit. It felt wrong, though, to spare them after all he knew they had to have done, the suffering they had imposed on countless girls and women.

Bolan had no more grenades, but he was willing to attempt a bluff. The soil around him was strewed with stones, and he chose one more or less the size and shape of a grenade. It called for expert aim to make it work, and Bolan managed it, winding up the pitch and letting fly from forty feet. The stone hit the driver's door, bounced once and then started to roll toward the forward wheel well, making ample noise along the way.

It was enough.

The two men charged out from behind the car and took off in opposite directions to escape what they supposed to be another hand grenade. The rifleman peeled off to Bolan's left, and since his weapon marked him as the greater danger, the Executioner tracked him with the MP-5 SD-3's sights, then rattled off half a dozen rounds to drop the soldier in his tracks.

And that left one.

The officer—which he had to have been, according to his uniform and armament—was running uphill, in the same direction that his miniconvoy had been headed when it went to hell. There was no way for him to know that he was moving ever closer to his executioner.

A 3-round burst ripped through the officer's tunic, spinning him, and three more parabellum rounds punched into him before he fell. His body shivered for a moment, as if stricken with a chill, and then was still.

Bolan double-checked the killing ground, then rose and walked down to the road. He turned right toward the curve, beyond which Maksimovic would—he hoped—be waiting with the truck and twenty-odd frightened passengers.

They had a long drive ahead, if they were to make the coast by sunrise.

3

Colonel Muhammad Herak had long since grown weary of waiting. In his case delays weren't merely tedious: they posed a clear and present danger for him and his men. If someone fingered them, and they were cornered by the Serbs...

The Muslim officer shrugged off his morbid thoughts and focused on the highway that would bring his contact west from Zvornik with the women. They were paramount in Herak's mind, the primary reason he'd agreed to join American intelligence officers in their bizarre globe-hopping scheme.

Herak didn't care what happened in the Netherlands, in Germany, or in America. His plate was heaped with enough problems, right there in Bosnia. His coreligionists were being slaughtered, and the constant rapes were part of it.

He understood that saving the women would make no real difference in his country's civil war. And they were "damaged goods," at that. All victims, innocent of any crime themselves, but to Muslim men, these women would be soiled, untouchable, beyond the pale for any serious relationship. A few of them, at least, would almost certainly be pregnant, and thus doubly cursed.

How could Herak, as a commander of the Islamic militia, help these women whose lives had been stolen away? He knew there was not much future for them in their native land. In towns and villages where Islam lived and breathed, a lot of men still insisted that their brides be virgins and their wives forever "loyal."

This collaboration with the Americans might help, somehow, although Herak still had his doubts. At least it was a chance to strike against his enemies, instead of simply hanging back in defensive positions and rolling with the punches. It wore a soldier down, the incessant shelling and harassment, hanging on to ground that would be worthless if and when they won the struggle.

Herak glanced at his watch, growing increasingly uneasy as the minutes ticked away. The deadline for their rendezvous had passed ten minutes earlier, and he wondered how much longer he should wait.

Three miles to the south, the town of Split was dark and silent, the local fishermen and farmers still asleep. They would be waking soon, however, to scratch their living from the sea or soil, somehow surviving in the face of poverty, privation, pestilence and civil war. Sometimes, he wondered how they managed.

Things could be worse though, he realized. The Serbs controlled two-thirds of Bosnia-Herzegovina, but for all their ruthless "ethnic cleansing," they were still not able to destroy the spirit of their Muslim enemies. If anything, adversity had forged the Islamic community into a united front unknown before the civil war broke out.

"How much longer, sir?"

Herak's lieutenant sounded nervous, fingering the safety on his automatic rifle while he scanned the empty road.

"Not long." Another ten or fifteen minutes, he decided, keeping the specifics to himself.

The words had barely left his lips when static crackled from the radio in his command vehicle. Herak's driver grabbed the dashboard-mounted microphone, then leaned forward to turn down the volume on the radio. After listening closely for a moment, the driver raised his head, then spoke directly to Herak.

"The scout, sir. He reports a truck approaching."

"Can he identify the driver?"

There was a hasty consultation. "He can't be sure, sir."

"Very well." Herak addressed his troops. "Stand ready!"

THE TOWN OF SPLIT WAS aptly named from Bolan's point of view. It was a place to leave from, to get away from Bosnia-Herzegovina and the brutal war that had become a fact of daily life.

But not just yet. He still had work to do before he put the war-torn land behind him and moved on to the next phase of his mission. Liberating Zvornik's Muslim hostages had been a good-faith gesture, the first step on a journey that would carry him across the European continent.

His final destination lay five hundred miles to the northwest—beyond the Alps, across four countries fronting the North Sea. He needed better field intelligence before he went directly to the source, and there were certain steps he had to follow if he meant to shut the pipeline down.

And Bolan planned to do exactly that.

"Five more miles, I think," Zeljko Maksimovic said, seeming perfectly at ease behind the wheel.

There had been nothing in the way of opposition since they'd cleared the killing ground outside Zvornik, but the fight had cost them precious time. Bolan could only hope that their contact had the courage to remain on station, take the extra risk to wait it out.

If not, he'd have to fall back on the secondary rendezvous, and that meant meeting after daybreak. That would multiply the danger ten times over, with the Serbs on full alert and mounting armed patrols.

Bolan glanced back through the open window to the covered truck bed where the women huddled on the wooden benches, and on the floor. But they didn't seem nearly as frightened as they'd been at Zvornik in captivity. Perhaps, Bolan thought, they'd reached a point where any change, however perilous, came as a relief.

They weren't going into the coastal town of Split. Maksimovic and his contact had arranged a meeting point outside, where they would theoretically be safe from prying eyes. He thought about the prospect of a double-cross and kept the MP-5 SD-3 submachine gun in his lap, the safety off, his right hand curled around the pistol grip.

Relaxing on a mission was the kind of error that could get a soldier killed.

He trusted his driver to a point, but there was still the possibility that Maksimovic's contacts, his superiors in the militia, might have a concealed agenda of their own. He understood their goals were different than his own, but the ongoing civil strife in Bosnia had given him a handle on his new campaign.

The traffic wasn't drugs or weapons this time. It was human beings.

And the problem, as stated to Bolan by Hal Brognola, stateside, was relatively straightforward. A drug-addicted prostitute in Amsterdam had killed herself almost two months earlier. When her ID and entry papers were identified as forgeries, a background search was instituted, and the dead woman was traced back to Visoko, in Bosnia-Herzegovina. The trace got shaky after that, but evidence—described by Interpol as eighty-five percent reliable—suggested that the woman was no willing transplant to the Netherlands. It seemed that she was one of several hundred Muslim women missing from the strife-torn country, presumed to be dead or confined to a Serbian brothel. Now Dutch authorities reported finding other prostitutes from Bosnia, all "missing" Muslims, in the red-light district of Amsterdam.

Compulsory prostitution had long been an unspoken blight on the Netherlands. Most of the victims, before the late eighties, had been sold to Dutch pimps by "recruiters" or impoverished parents in Asia or Latin America. They added "color" to the legalized brothels that operated freely in commercial red-light zones from Groningen to Haarlem and The Hague. Since the collapse of Russian communism and the destruction of the Berlin Wall, however, there had been a swing toward Eastern European girls and women—Poles, Czechs, Slavs. According to investigators, the majority were lured from villages and farms with promises of lucrative employment, education, fame and fortune.

From time to time though, other windows of opportunity presented themselves. It had happened in Beirut, in Bogotá, in Belfast, and, most recently, in Bosnia. Life was cheap, dead bodies plentiful, and missing persons had a way of being forgotten. It was no great challenge to abduct a woman—or a dozen women—shoot her up with drugs until she craved the needle and "break her in" with rape around the clock until no act of degradation came as a surprise.

"The contact," Maksimovic said suddenly.

Bolan spotted several vehicles up ahead around which could be seen the silhouettes of armed men.

"I hope so."

Even as he spoke, he weighed the compact submachine gun in his hands.

THE RISK, FOR MAKSIMOVIC, was a matter of degree. He'd been living in the middle of a war zone for the past four years painfully aware that his side was outnumbered by a ruthless enemy. He'd been fired on countless times and wounded twice. At least three men had died by his hand.

Maksimovic had no reason to mistrust his leaders in the present operation, but experience had taught him to be wary. As he drove toward the rendezvous, he knew there was at least a possibility that someone other than the colonel would be waiting for him.

At his side, the man who called himself Belasko seemed immune to fear. From his demeanor and his performance in the recent battle, Maksimovic knew the American had faced death a thousand times and come away the victor.

After a moment, Maksimovic felt his apprehension fading. He picked out familiar uniforms and flashed his headlights once, just long enough to recognize the colonel's round, impassive face in the glare.

"It's okay," he told Bolan, braking to a halt and switching off the engine. There was no sound now, except for boots on gravel as the colonel's men spread out to flank the truck, their weapons ready to meet any enemy threat.

Maksimovic found the inside latch and opened his door, stepping down to greet the colonel with a tired salute.

"The women?" Colonel Herak asked without preamble.

"In the back, sir."

Bolan joined them, circling the cab, his submachine gun dangling from a sling across one shoulder. Herak switched to English for the American's convenience.

"You're late. Was there a problem?"

"We had company," Bolan answered. "They didn't make it."

"Soldiers?"

"They had guns and uniforms."

"You killed them?"

He didn't answer. The silence hung between them until the colonel cleared his throat. He turned to the short lieutenant standing just behind him.

"Make sure the women are...unharmed." The last word almost seemed to choke him. He turned back to Maksimovic with his usual stern expression. "Are you ready to leave at once?" he asked.

"Yes, sir. We might need some fuel if we have far to go."

Herak snapped his fingers at a chunky sergeant. "Fuel!" he ordered. "Right now."

"You're going north, to Skradin," he said to Maksimovic. "You'll be expected there."

"Yes, sir."

The land surrounding Skradin was controlled by Muslims, one of three small enclaves in the country where they held a majority. The women would be safe there.

Maksimovic turned to the American, his hand extended. "Go with God."

"If he wants to tag along," Bolan said, smiling, "I don't mind."

COLONEL HERAK LED Mack Bolan off to one side as the truck pulled out and disappeared, northbound.

"You kept your word," Herak said.

"You sound surprised."

"In truth I am. The odds against you were extreme."

"We made it back."

"And now it's time for what you call the payoff. I have the information you required."

"I'm listening," the Executioner replied.

"It is a fact that women, Muslim women, have been taken from the country and sold like cattle."

"I knew that coming in."

"But you required a name for the broker."

"Right."

"The man you seek is Borislav Sestic, a black-hearted Serbian jackal. He has close friends in the Chetniks—the Serb paramilitary unit—and among the leaders of the so-called Serb Republic. Perhaps Karadzic."

Karan Karadzic was the mouthpiece for the Serb Republic and an outspoken proponent of "ethnic cleansing." He'd been denounced as a war criminal in the United Nations and by much of the world's press.

"Is there any word on his connections?" Bolan asked.

"You mean in Amsterdam?"

"Ideally, yes."

"Unfortunately not. I have no doubt that Sestic could provide the names if only he was willing," Herak told him.

"It's a thought."

"Within the country, we believe he works with Slobodan Ribnica, a commander of the Serb militia based at Banja Luka, to the north. Ribnica makes no secret of the way his soldiers use our women. He's proud of the atrocities, as if they guarantee his place in Paradise."

"I know the type."

"We've tried to kill Ribnica several times, but his life is—how do you say it—charmed?"

"That's how we say it," Bolan replied dryly.

"He is favored by the devil. It sounds like superstition, but I believe it. Our soldiers once stopped his motorcade outside Zinica. Thirteen men were killed, nine of them Serbs. As for Ribnica, bullets pierced his clothing, here and here." The colonel touched his own shirt, left and right. "He escaped without a scratch. Without a scratch!"

"Could be he's used up all his luck."

"He has a devil watching over him," Herak said again.

"This Borislav Sestic," Bolan said. "Where do I find him?"

"He makes his home in Bileca," the colonel replied. "Perhaps two hundred kilometers to the southeast."

"I'll need some transportation. Without the truck—"

"Much too conspicuous, my friend. You need a car, but nothing obvious. In Bosnia, new cars belong to politicians and observers sent by the United Nations to report on how we die. You need a small car, older, with some superficial damage."

"Suits me, as long as it's got something underneath the hood. I could also use some food." Bolan thought about the trip in front of him—125 miles, give or take—and tried to weigh the odds. "And a map, in English, if you've got it."

"I have something better," Herak said. "You will take a guide."

An alarm went off in Bolan's head.

"Do you have somebody who speaks English?"

"Yes, indeed." The colonel tapped a thumb against his burly chest. "I speak your language well, yes?"

Bolan nodded. "Can they spare you here?"

"The war is everywhere. If helping you can strike a blow against our enemies and save lives, it will be worth the effort."

"I was thinking of the risk," Bolan said.

"I am still a soldier, even if my rank excludes direct participation in combat."

"That could change if you come along with me."

"I will be prepared."

"Okay. When do we leave?"

"The car is ready," Herak answered. "I will get some clothes for me, and then we shall go."

If nothing else, it would be an interesting drive, Bolan thought. He only hoped it wouldn't turn out to be one-way.

4

The villa near Bileca had remained more or less unscathed by four long years of civil war. There were some bullet scars around the outer walls, but that was unavoidable. And on one occasion a guard had gotten drunk and emptied half a magazine from his Kalashnikov into the living room, but the damage had long since been repaired. As for the trigger-happy guard... Well, he was simply *gone*.

Discipline was important to Borislav Sestic. Long before the fighting started, when the various nearby republics constituted greater Yugoslavia, he'd been known—to everyone who counted—as a reliable, discreet, productive businessman. That meant he kept his house in order, made the necessary payoffs promptly and without complaint and cleaned up his own mess, quietly, whenever there were problems he couldn't have foreseen.

It made no difference, for the most part, that his stock-in-trade was banned by law. Sestic had been pimping women since the age of thirteen when he began to "manage business" for his sixteen-year-old sister, Tascha. She was dead now—from an overdose of drugs—but she had only been the first of many. Once his reputation was established in the business, it was easy. Third World countries placed a premium on sons, and it was no great challenge to obtain attractive girls at bargain rates. The best ones went into Sestic's brothels, while the rest were sold again to associates outside the country. Now, with something close to anarchy enveloping his homeland, Sestic's resourcefulness took over. It pleased him to steal Muslim women from the countryside, sell them abroad and know that he had done his part for ethnic cleansing.

It was still illegal, of course, but that was another good thing about war: established rules flew out the window.

Business. Pleasure. Politics. Who could say where the dividing line was drawn?

Such fine points didn't trouble Sestic. He kept both eyes firmly focused on the profit motive, with a sidelong glance toward personal amusement, now and then, when a new shipment was received. He didn't bother with the details of conditioning his stock these days, but left that chore to his subordinates.

Awakened by a rumbling sound, Sestic lay in bed and listened to the distant crashing of artillery around Trebinje, twenty miles southwest of Bileca. The Muslims would be cringing in their holes. It amused him, picturing the bloody chaos in his mind, and for a moment Sestic wished that he could hop into his Mercedes-Benz and drive out to watch the shelling for awhile.

But if the past four years had taught him anything, it had to be that it was safer doing business in the shadows, well behind the lines of battle. He wasn't afraid of killing, if the odds were on his side, but there was nothing to be gained from walking into danger as if he were invincible.

He kept a team of guards around the villa, armed men on watch around the clock, three shifts per day. The job wasn't demanding, and he paid them well enough to guarantee their loyalty. Thus far, the guards hadn't been called upon to fight, but they were handpicked killers from the slaughterhouses of Garazde, Sarajevo and Mostar.

One thing about the new republic: there was no shortage of young men with blood on their hands.

Sestic checked the clock beside his bed and saw that it was nearly dawn. Too early for a man of leisure to begin his day. He shifted in the king-size bed and fluffed up the pillows to make himself more comfortable. He had no reason to believe that Death was coming for him as the night bled into dawn.

THE BATTERED CAR HAD a paint job that resembled urban camouflage, with primer spots and rusty blotches overlapping paint that was a faded, washed-out green. One hubcap of the four originals was still in place, defaced by scars, while rust had taken over on the other wheels. The headlights were a trifle cross-eyed, but it made no difference since the car was running dark.

Colonel Herak nosed into a stand of trees and killed the engine. "It's fifty yards that way," he said, pointing through the trees in the direction of their target. "I should come with you, perhaps."

"I'd rather have you here and ready with the car," Bolan replied. "When I bring him out, there won't be any time to spare."

"As you wish."

What Bolan didn't say—and what Herak should have known without an explanation—was that they were total strangers when it came to fighting styles and signals, the intuitive cooperation that was necessary for a combat team. A misstep could get them killed, and Bolan still had too far to go before his mission was completed.

"Are you sure this guy speaks English?" Bolan asked.

"Plus Russian, French and German. Borislav Sestic might be a monster but he's not a fool."

"As long as he can understand me when I tell him where to go and what to do."

Beyond that point, the Executioner decided, he'd let his hardware do the talking.

Bolan went in through the trees, his nightsuit and the camo warpaint helping him blend in with the shadows. Dawn was fast approaching, but it would still be dark among the trees when Bolan reached the villa. The sentries would be letting down their guard as sunrise approached, a reflex built into the human species from the days when man was more at home in caves and trees. A savvy warrior who could take advantage of that built-in lull was points ahead.

He reached the eight-foot wall, checked briefly for alarms and sensors, then scaled it in a rush. The grounds were thick with decorative trees and shrubs, assisting Bolan as he moved in the direction of the house. He'd covered half the distance before he met an armed sentry. He closed in from the soldier's blind side, leading with the SMG until its muzzle almost grazed his target's shoulder. Bolan had the weapon set for semiauto fire, and when he squeezed the trigger, one round slammed into the watchman's skull.

The guard went down without a whimper, and Bolan stepped around him, moving on. A moment later he'd reached the open lawn, where he spotted two more sentries. One was on his left, roughly forty feet away, and had his back turned toward him. On Bolan's right and facing him, another gunman walked his beat.

After flicking the subgun's fire selector to 3-round bursts, the warrior took the gunner facing him. He lined up his shot from thirty feet and stroked the trigger. Bolan didn't wait to see the rounds strike, but swiveled toward the second guard, squeezing off another burst before the man had opportunity to register the muffled sound of gunfire, turn around and seek its source.

Three down, and while Bolan didn't have a clue how many troops were on the grounds, his runway to the house was now clear. A short sprint through the first gray light of dawn, and he flattened up against the southern wall. He began to work his way around the house until he found an unlocked door.

It seemed to be a service entrance, apparently open for the guards in case they needed access to the kitchen, where a coffeepot sat steaming on a hot plate. Bolan made his way silently from room to room. He met no resistance as he gravitated toward the bedrooms on the second floor. If there were gunners in the house, they had to be sleeping on the job.

In fact he found that was exactly right. The first upstairs door Bolan tried, he found three men snoring in their bunks. He took a moment to rap the butt of his subgun against the men's temples, before removing plastic cuffs from a pouch on his web belt and securing their hands.

In another bedroom, three more sleepers received the same treatment. The next two rooms he checked were empty.

That left one.

The Executioner slipped across the threshold and saw his sleeping quarry. Three strides brought him to Sestic's bed where he bent down to whip back the covers. He clamped his hand over Sestic's mouth and pressed the muzzle of his weapon between the pimp's eyes.

"They tell me you speak English."

It took a moment until his quarry nodded, blinking rapidly as if to punctuate the silent message.

"Good. Now listen carefully. I've killed to get this far. Do you want to live?"

Sestic nodded, his lips dry against Bolan's palm.

"Okay. I'm stepping back. Get up and do exactly as you're told. No sudden moves, no noise. A blind man couldn't miss you at this range."

Bolan took a long step backward from the bed and waited, covering the pimp as he stood, a paunchy little man in silk pajamas.

"I want both hands on your head, and lock your fingers."

Sestic followed the orders, moving out as Bolan wagged his submachine gun's muzzle toward the open door. When he was two steps from the threshold, the big American stopped him.

"Hold it there."

He stepped around his captive, peered into the corridor and found it empty. Bolan led the way and held his weapon ready as he motioned for Sestic to follow.

"Come ahead. We're going down the stairs."

Sestic walked like a robot, plodding mechanically toward the staircase. Bolan followed close enough to nail Sestic if his hostage tried to bolt, but far enough removed that Sestic couldn't reach the submachine gun with a sudden grab.

They were halfway down the stairs when one of Sestic's gunmen stepped out of the living room. He glanced up toward the staircase, blinking at the sight of his employer with the black-clad warrior bringing up the rear.

The gunner tried to swing up his automatic rifle, but he got tangled in the sling, and it was all the edge Mack Bolan needed. He leaned across the banister and fired a 3-round burst. The parabellum shockers stitched neat holes across the sentry's chest and slammed him backward onto an ornate coffee table.

The noise was loud enough to rouse the house, if any other occupants were still alive, and Bolan gave his prisoner a shove in the direction of the hallway leading to the service entrance.

"That way. Hurry up."

Daylight was coming on as Bolan reached the yard and prodded Sestic out in front of him. The trees seemed almost close enough to touch, but they'd have to cross the open ground before they came to any shelter. They were nearly there when Bolan heard a shout behind him. He turned to find a sentry closing on them from the southwest corner of the house. As Bolan watched, the soldier brought an AK-47 to his shoulder, lining up the shot.

The range was sixty feet or so, no picnic for a snap shot with an SMG, but Bolan gave it everything he had. It took the last half of his weapon's magazine on full-auto, and hot rounds stuttered through the suppressor, drilling Bolan's target as the soldier fired a short burst of his own. The AK's rounds went high and wide, and the gunner dropped like a scarecrow with the brace removed. The echo of his adversary's gunfire traveled back and forth between the house and trees.

"Get moving!"

Bolan gave the pimp a hard shove toward the highway, following immediately on his heels. Reloading on the move, he listened for the sound of pursuit, but heard nothing further from the house.

They reached the outer wall of the estate. Sestic stood, bewildered, gaping at the wall that loomed almost a yard above his balding head.

"I can't do this," he blurted.

"You'd be surprised."

A chopping gesture with the SMG sent Bolan's captive scrambling up the wall, his fingers scrabbling at the cinder blocks on top. He started to slide back, but Bolan was behind him, lending muscle to shove Sestic over and beyond the barrier. Then the Executioner touched down beside him, reaching out to drag his captive upright.

"Please, my leg," Sestic began to whine.

"If you can't run, I'll have to shoot you."

Bolan smiled grimly at Sestic's recovery as they took off.

THE SOUND OF GUNFIRE startled Colonel Herak, but he stayed in the car, clutching a folding-stock AK-74 with the barrel cut back to ten inches in length, for the equivalent of a 5.56 mm submachine gun.

He watched the clock and tried to calculate how long it would take for Belasko to retrace his steps with a reluctant prisoner in tow. Five minutes? Ten? Within a quarter of an hour, maybe less, full daylight would expose Herak to any passing enemies. If hostile troops came out in force, he'd be forced to flee or fight, with neither option offering much prospect for success. The wise decision, he couldn't help thinking, would be to evacuate the scene right now and save himself.

But honor called for him to stay where he was, no matter what the cost.

Two minutes later he heard a thrashing from the woods in front of him. Belasko had been silent when he'd disappeared among the trees, but it was always different when a soldier had to run for safety. Sestic, more than likely, would be making his share of the noise.

Or it could be gunmen from the villa, closing in.

Herak opened the driver's door, stepped out and braced his sawed-off rifle on the windowsill. His finger tightened on the trigger, taking up the slack, prepared to spray the woods with bullets if an enemy appeared.

But it was Sestic who came reeling through the trees, his silk pajamas torn around one knee, a button missing from the top. His feet were bare and bleeding from the long run through the woods. Behind him, the big American was a looming shadow.

Herak had the back door open, waiting for them, when they reached the car. Belasko shoved the pimp inside and forced him to the floorboard, then crawled in behind him. Herak closed the door, slid in behind the wheel and twisted the ignition key.

"We need somewhere to talk," Bolan said, "with no interruptions."

The colonel smiled and wheeled the car back onto the highway.

"I know just the place," he said.

THE FARM LAY WEST of Stolac, long abandoned when the residents departed in the face of Serb advances. Battle lines had drifted back and forth since then, but the original inhabitants hadn't returned.

The barn was large enough for several cars. Bright daylight streamed through an open loft hatch by the time they parked inside and closed the double doors behind them. Sestic had recovered somewhat from his ordeal at the villa, but his fear was evident as Bolan pulled him from the car. Speaking English seemed to place him under even greater strain.

"Who are you?" the pimp asked. "What do you want from me?"

"Ideally," Bolan said, "I'd like to squash you like an insect. As it is, you might just have a chance to change my mind."

"To live? What can I do?"

"I need some information."

Sestic seemed to have some trouble with the concept, frowning as he stood before his captors, shifting his weight from one foot to the other.

"What sort of information?" he asked.

"You sell women out of the country," Bolan said. "That's common knowledge."

"What you suggest is—"

"Absolutely true," Bolan cut him off. "You're burning up what little time you might have left."

"If I was selling women—"

"You would need a contact," Bolan finished for him. "That's my question. They wind up in Amsterdam. We know that, too. Is there a middleman?"

"There is no one I know in Amsterdam," the pimp replied.

"I'll take that as a yes. Who takes the women off your hands?"

"They go to Germany."

"That's *where,* not *who.*"

"There is a man...."

He hesitated, stalling, and the submachine gun stuttered briefly, raising spurts of dust at Sestic's feet. The pimp flinched, almost losing his balance.

"Don't kill me! Please!"

"I'm running out of patience. Does he have a name, or not?" Bolan barked.

"Hans Kettering," Sestic replied, almost sobbing.

"Where's his headquarters?"

Sestic blinked rapidly. "I do not understand."

"Where does he live? His base of operations?" Bolan snapped.

"I have never been to Germany," he stated, as if that answered anything.

The SMG came up to hold a bead on Sestic's nose. "Try once more," Bolan suggested, tightening his trigger finger.

"Stuttgart!" Sestic gasped. "The number, when I call him, is in Stuttgart. I can't tell you where he lives. I only met him once, and he came here... I mean, to Sarajevo."

"That's convenient."

"He was checking out the merchandise."

Behind him, Bolan heard Herak snarl, a muffled sound of fury.

"This Kettering," Bolan said. "I assume he represents a syndicate?"

Sestic shrugged. "I assume as much."

"How are the women sent to Germany?"

"There are different ways." Their hostage seemed a bit more stable now that he was talking business. "Some, we send the long way around, by boat. A steamer takes them from Dubrovnik or Zadar and drops them off at Bremerhaven, even Homburg. Sometimes, we use a bus, going through Austria to Munich. Once there was a charter flight, but now things are too unstable, with air traffic and the war."

The Executioner didn't expect specific details of deliveries from Sestic, who would almost certainly have satisfied himself with cash in hand, the details parceled out to his subordinates and those in Germany who took delivery of the women.

It was a stepping-stone, at least. With any luck his contacts in the States could flesh things out, provide him with a better handle on the German situation.

Colonel Herak's voice broke the momentary silence. "You work for Slobodan Ribnica, don't you?"

Sestic swallowed and tried to find his voice. "I don't know what you mean."

"Oh, no? Do you deny collusion with the Serbian militia to abduct our women from the countryside and sell them into slavery?"

"I don't... I... What..."

The hostage glanced at Bolan with something that might have been a plea for help.

"I'm finished here," Bolan said to Herak.

"So am I."

The pistol shot slammed Sestic backward onto the earthen floor. It was a clean shot, right between the eyes, and the man was dead before he hit the ground. The next half-dozen shots were more like therapy.

"All done?" he asked the colonel.

"For the moment."

"We should go," Bolan said. "I have one or two things left to do before I fly to Germany."

"I'd like to help you," Herak offered.

"Suits me," the Executioner replied. "Let's go."

5

From Slobodan Ribnica's point of view, the war was going fairly well. Of course, he'd have much preferred a swift and easy victory, but there was something to be said about a protracted conflict. If the Muslims had surrendered quickly, ethnic cleansing would have been retarded, maybe canceled altogether. It was difficult enough to run the concentration camps and hide the evidence of massacres in active combat zones, with the Red Cross, United Nations and a host of other busybodies horning in on Serbian affairs. If there was peace, Ribnica knew that weeding out the Muslim traitors would be much more difficult.

Ribnica tried to keep specific records for his district, but the task was overwhelming. Every day, patrols went out, artillery barrages were directed at the enemy and more girls and women were transported to the camps and brothels where they served the Serbian Republic on their backs and on their knees. The body counts were often estimated—and, Ribnica realized, sometimes fabricated—but he did his best to keep the books of death.

And on the side he kept a second set of books, recording his personal profits from the spoils of war.

Borislav Sestic deserved credit for taking a simple idea and turning it into gold.

They had been collecting women for almost a year, when Sestic sent one of his underlings to Ribnica's headquarters with an enticing business proposition. Since Muslim women had been marked for exploitation as a part of ethnic cleansing, what would it matter if a handful disappeared from Bosnia each month or two? In Western Europe there were syndicates that paid hard cash for prostitutes from other countries. As it happened, the new market opened up around the same time that political upheavals and resurgent fundamentalism closed some traditional outlets in the Middle East.

It was a seller's market at the moment, and a man with merchandise on tap could make a fortune overnight. So far, the system had been working well for Ribnica. His superiors were none the wiser, and if his calculations were correct, he'd be able to retire from military service in a year or less.

Ribnica faced the huge map tacked to the wall of his study, frowning at the colored markers indicating Serbian and Muslim positions. As it stood, the Serbs controlled about two-thirds of Bosnia, and they were gaining ground slowly, day by day. If the Americans refrained from meddling, another year could see the work completed and Slobodan Ribnica left with no real mission to pursue. It would be good, he thought, to have a nest egg waiting for him in his numbered Swiss account.

The field command post outside Banja Luka was a comfortable place, all things considered. Ribnica had an air conditioner that often worked, a swimming pool that only leaked a little and the relative security of having troops around him.

This day, like every other, would belong to men with strength enough to seize their object or desire and hold it fast. When Ribnica wanted something he reached out and took it... or dispatched his troops to do the job on his behalf.

THEY PARKED THE CAR half a mile from Ribnica's field command post and hiked overland through fields that had once been cultivated but were now overgrown with weeds that reached almost to shoulder height. Bolan had traded in his nightsuit for a set of camouflage fatigues, while Herak wore an olive-drab jacket, blue jeans and a faded denim shirt. The colonel carried his sawed-off AK-74, and a Walther P-5 semiauto pistol was leathered on his hip. Spare magazines for the rifle were slung across his chest in a khaki bandoleer. Both men were also packing smoke and frag grenades.

Their strategy had been determined in advance, with sketches of the Serbian command post drawn by Muslim agents in the field. Bolan kept the conversation to a minimum as they approached their target through the open fields. He knew Herak well enough by now that they were able to communicate with basic hand signals or a few brief words.

With any luck it would be enough to get them through.

The spotters estimated that twenty-five or thirty soldiers—Ribnica's private bodyguards—were on the premises at any given time. It made for long odds, but Bolan had been faced with worse, and he'd survived.

They reached the outer limits of the compound twenty minutes after starting out. There was no fence around the grounds, but two watchtowers, close to twenty feet in height, had been erected to the north and east, with interlocking fields of fire for light machine guns. The compound buildings were collected in a circle, thirty-five or forty yards across, with Ribnica's CP as the centerpiece. The flag of Bosnia-Herzegovina, a blue shield on a field of white, snapped fitfully against a breeze that blew in from the south. From what Bolan took to be the mess hall, a metal chimney wafted smoke that carried the smell of food. He counted nine uniformed men on the ground, all packing small arms on their hips or in their hands.

"Those towers have to go," he told Herak.

"I agree. I'll take the farther one."

"Good," Bolan said. "Is ten minutes long enough to get yourself in place?"

"I think so."

"I'll move when you do, then. Good luck."

Before Herak was out of sight, Bolan had already selected his jumping-off point for the raid. He needed altitude to reach the gunner in his lookout tower, and he chose a tree roughly fifty feet due north of the elevated sniper's nest. It was a fairly easy climb once he'd leaped to reach the lowest sturdy branch, with ferns and loam beneath him when he had to jump.

Three minutes brought Bolan to a perch that would be adequate for his purposes. He had the shot lined up a moment later, the tower sentry's profile clearly framed in his submachine gun's sights. He waited for the rest of their agreed-upon time to elapse, his finger curled around the trigger. He didn't know exactly what Herak had in mind, but since the colonel didn't possess a silencer, it stood to reason that his move would rouse the camp.

Bolan knew that stealth could take them only so far on a daylight raid. He was prepared to face his enemies on equal terms—if it could be called that—with odds of twelve or fifteen men to one.

He flinched involuntarily when Herak's grenade went off. The tower sentry pivoted to face the fireball, showing Bolan his back. A short burst from the SMG drilled into his shoulder blades, and Bolan's target toppled forward in a clumsy high dive from the tower, legs flailing as he fell.

The rest of it would have to happen on the ground, and Bolan made his move from his position in the tree. His legs absorbed the impact of the drop then from a practiced shoulder roll he was up and running toward the killing ground.

THE FRAG GRENADE HAD BEEN a judgment call. Herak's angle of attack was poor with the Kalashnikov, and he'd scored a bull's-eye with his pitch.

It was a short dash to the nearest building, which he took to be some kind of storage shed. He spent a moment crouching in its shadow, listening to the sounds of automatic weapons from the far side of the camp, then stepped out of cover, seeking human targets.

On Herak's left two soldiers moved toward the nearest tower, their eyes fixed on the shattered lookout's nest. The closer man spotted Herak as he emerged from cover. He snapped a warning to his comrade, who stopped short to bring the stranger under fire.

It was too late.

The cut-down rifle stuttered, spewing empty brass. Herak's targets jerked through a crazy little dance before dropping in their tracks. One lay unmoving where he fell, the other writhed briefly, like a lizard with a broken back, before he, too, was still.

Herak made a break for what he knew to be the communications hut, intent on blocking any signal that would summon reinforcements to the camp. He wasn't challenged as he crossed the ten or fifteen yards of open ground to reach his destination, flattening himself against the nearest wall. On the count of three he eased around the corner, leading with his weapon.

A soldier emerged from the hut's open doorway, and Herak squeezed off a 3-round burst at point-blank range. The impact slammed the soldier backward, across the threshold and into the hut. He struck a chair on rollers, and it scooted out from under him, colliding with a metal desk before it came to rest. The lifeless body sprawled in front of Herak, but it no longer held any interest for him. The radio and fax machine were now the colonel's concern. He directed a sweeping burst from left to right, the steel-jacketed projectiles drilling glass, aluminum and plastic.

He was finished in a moment and turned back in the direction of the door. A shadow fell across his field of vision. Herak was ready for him. He brought the stubby muzzle of his weapon chopping down against the soldier's gun hand. The Serb—a sergeant, by his stripes—cried out in pain and staggered backward.

The short Kalashnikov rapped out a 4-round burst that punched him over onto his back, heels drumming on the sod before his life ran out.

Herak put the communications hut behind him and went out to join the battle.

THE CAMP HAD BEEN constructed to protect Commander Slobodan Ribnica, but it felt more like a prison now. He peered out through a window of his sleeping quarters and saw two bodies stretched out on the ground almost fifty feet away. A fire was burning—presumably the source of the explosion that had awakened him—but he couldn't make out which building was in flames.

It was definitely time to go.

Ribnica dressed in seconds flat, one thing he'd learned from military life. His top priority was speed, to get away before his enemies had a chance to pin him down.

There was no doubt in Ribnica's mind that the attackers sought to trap him and to destroy him for his role in punishing Muslim vermin. He offered no apologies for any orders he'd given in performance of his duties. As for any profits he collected on the side, well, that was private, and the world at large didn't have to know.

Someone was calling to him from the office portion of his quarters, and it took a moment, in his panic, for Ribnica to identify the voice of Major Vojslav Silajdzic, his second in command. There was a tremor in the major's voice, but that could be excitement just as easily as fear.

"We need to hurry, sir!"

Ribnica opened the door that stood between them, stepping out to join Silajdzic as he buckled on his pistol belt. "We need a vehicle."

"Of course, sir. If you'll follow me..."

Ribnica noted for the first time that Silajdzic had an automatic rifle in his hand. The thought of fighting clear, from what had been his private stronghold, frightened Ribnica, but he put the fear behind him, forced it back into a corner of his mind where such things waited for consideration at a more convenient time.

Survival. He'd snatched that precious gift from others, did it frequently enough that he knew all the moves by heart. It cut both ways.

The explosive sounds of combat rushed to meet Ribnica as Silajdzic opened the door. Cordite stung his nostrils. He heard the snap-snap-snap of bullets flying and saw one of his soldiers fall, gut shot, to rise no more.

The motor pool lay to their right, eighty yards away across open ground. Once they began to run, there'd be nothing in the way of cover to protect them. Only speed, agility and nerve would matter then. Ribnica wished briefly he'd kept himself in better shape.

He drew his pistol and was encouraged by the solid weight of the weapon in his hand. Whatever else he might have lost in terms of physical conditioning, Ribnica still possessed a marksman's eye.

"Now!"

The order from Silajdzic cut into the commander's thoughts and snapped him back to cold reality. Another heartbeat and he was sprinting on the major's heels in the direction of the motor pool. Ribnica saw the vehicles, undamaged, waiting for them underneath a camo netting braced on wooden poles.

Sounds of combat assaulted Ribnica's eardrums. Something blew, and the heat and shock wave from the blast propelled him to even greater speed. Three or four long strides in front of him, Silajdzic ducked his head and kept on running, both hands gripping his Kalashnikov.

They ran directly to Ribnica's staff car, passing several trucks and two jeeps mounting .50-caliber machine guns. Ribnica didn't plan to challenge the attackers on his own. If his selected team of bodyguards couldn't repulse the enemy, another gun or two would make no difference to the outcome of the battle. It was better for the officer in charge to save himself, regroup with other troops and come back to eliminate the enemy who dared to challenge him.

But first he had to make it out alive.

Ribnica climbed into the shotgun seat, Silajdzic at the wheel. The engine roared to life with one touch of the starter, and Silajdzic shifted into first.

"Hang on, sir!"

"Never mind hang on," Ribnica snapped. "Just get us out of here."

A BULLET WHINED PAST Bolan's head and sent him diving to a prone position, scanning for a target. Three Serbs were closing in on him, double-timing from the general direction of a barracks to his left. They were intent on pinning Bolan down, excitement overriding caution as they tried to close the gap.

He met them with a burst that tracked from left to right, 9 mm parabellum rounds exploding into flesh and bone. The runners stumbled, reeling, two of them colliding as they fell. Almost before they hit the ground, the warrior was on his feet and running hard toward Ribnica's quarters.

The sounds of battle on the far side of the camp told him Herak had been spotted and marked by the Serbs. Bolan wished him luck, but could offer no help at the moment. Ribnica was the target, and if a diversion helped him reach the camp commander, Bolan didn't mean to throw the opportunity away.

The number of enemies had been cut down, but they weren't home free yet. Before he reached Ribnica's quarters, Bolan knew that he could still lose out and see his quarry slip away. The whole point of their raid at Banja Luka was to shut down the slavers' pipeline, or damage it so badly that supply was interdicted while he crushed the middlemen and paid a hellfire visit to the marketplace.

But he'd have to take it one step at a time.

The front door to Ribnica's quarters was ajar when Bolan got there, and he shouldered through at once, the submachine gun tracking, seeking targets. Thirty seconds told him there was no one home, and Bolan doubled back to the entryway. He scanned the yard and was quick enough to glimpse two runners—one of them Ribnica—as they reached the motor pool and piled into a staff car. There was no time to waste.

Bolan made his stand between the staff car and the access road that would allow Ribnica to escape through Banja Luka, if he got that far. The Executioner waited, a fresh mag ready in the SMG, the stock braced solidly against his shoulder.

At a range of fifty yards, the driver had him spotted. There was room to swing around a man-sized obstacle, but Bolan's adversary was plainly not in the mood for detours. He aimed the car at Bolan like a manned projectile, racing toward him with the engine screaming.

Bolan aimed his first half-dozen rounds directly at the driver's face, ignoring Ribnica for the moment. Then he dropped his sights a fraction, squeezing off a long burst through the staff car's grille. A stream of rusty-looking water spouted from the radiator, and the hood blew backward as a bullet clipped the latch.

The staff car swerved off course. Bolan tracked it past him. Seconds later he was ready when the camo-painted charger plowed into Ribnica's quarters, clocking forty miles per hour.

The engine died on impact, but momentum bore the staff car forward, through Ribnica's outer office. It finally jolted to a halt against some filing cabinets on the wall that separated the commander's private quarters from the office space.

Bolan was close behind the car, closing in as Ribnica's door creaked open and the shaken commandant emerged, his face blood-streaked. He wore a holster, empty now, but the Executioner wasn't about to let him find another weapon. Fifteen feet separated them when Ribnica, blinking rapidly and swiping at the blood that smeared his face saw his adversary. He dropped to his knees and groped around, as if searching for a weapon. Bolan held down the trigger and sprayed Ribnica with the final bullets from his magazine.

He swiveled at the sound of footsteps behind him, bringing up the Desert Eagle automatic from its holster, lining up the shot.

"Don't shoot!" Herak was braced for sudden death, one hand outstretched, as if he thought his palm could stop the Magnum round. "We're finished here, I think."

"What about the others?" Bolan asked.

"Dead or running for their lives. They seem to think they're surrounded," Herak said.

"Works for me," the Executioner replied.

"It's time for us to go."

6

"What is the news?" Gunter Jodl asked, sipping schnapps and observing his subordinate almost casually.

Hans Kettering was clearly agitated. He squirmed in the heavy wooden chair that had been chosen with an eye toward keeping Jodl's visitors from getting too relaxed.

"We have been seriously damaged," Kettering replied. His crew cut showed his scalp on top, and he appeared to be lost inside a suit that was at least two sizes too large for him.

"Give me details."

"The pimp Borislav Sestic has been abducted," Kettering said, "and we assume he's dead. Whoever snatched him also shot up several of his men."

"He's not the only pimp in Bosnia," Jodl said, punctuating his remark with yet another sip of schnapps.

"The officer is dead, as well, Slobodan Ribnica," Kettering added.

"They were together?"

"No, sir. There were several hours between the two attacks. Enough for members of a strike force to transport themselves from one site to the next."

"You feel the two attacks are linked, then?"

"Yes, sir."

"Even with the constant violence in Bosnia? These men were not without their enemies."

"I don't trust coincidence," Kettering said.

"Nor I. What do you intend to do?"

"Stand watch, for now. Find out if those who killed Ribnica and Sestic are satisfied. They might ignore us, settle for the Serbs. If not, we have a better chance to beat them on familiar ground."

"That seems sensible," Jodl said. "Are your people ready?"

"They have been informed of the latest developments. Without a definite target, though, it is pointless to cover the airports, much less the highways. I can field a shooting team on fifteen minutes' notice."

"Fair enough. I trust it won't be necessary."

However, Gunter Jodl was far from convinced that their troubles were over. Granted, in a giant crazy house like Bosnia, it was impossible to say with any certainty exactly who was killing whom. Ironically the same chaotic situation that enabled him to purchase whores from Sestic and his military cohorts stymied any chance for Jodl to identify their killers from a distance.

Losing his connection was an inconvenience, but he had no doubt that new arrangements could be made. A greater problem, at the moment, lay in the reaction of his customers in Holland. They were men who paid top dollar for specific merchandise, and they weren't averse to raising hell if things went wrong. It would be inconvenient—costly, too—if Jodl lost their business. Worse, if they suspected treachery, it could mean war.

Jodl had no fear of being stalked around Cologne by Muslim troops from Bosnia. If it came down to that, he could protect himself. But first he had to find out what was happening, determine what the true risks were. And, in the process, he'd have to try to reassure his buyers in the Netherlands.

The danger he could deal with. Jodl's driving force was loss of all that he had worked for through the years. He had invested too much sweat and blood to simply let it slide, and if the blood had mostly come from others, well, that simply meant he was a survivor.

An enemy who tried to take him here, on his home ground, was in for a surprise. He, or they, wouldn't live long enough to learn from their mistake.

"I want your people on alert," he said to Kettering. "Beginning now."

"Yes, sir."

"And let me know if you hear anything at all."

"Of course."

"That's all. Dismissed."

Alone once more, Jodl sat and focused on the nameless, faceless enemy.

MACK BOLAN COULD HAVE flown from Sarajevo, but it would have meant backtracking for a hundred miles on old, war-damaged roads, to wait in line with refugees, reporters and United Nations personnel.

As an alternative, Herak had arranged a helicopter flight from Split to Mulat Island in the Adriatic, where a private plane was waiting for the lift to Austria. His pilot dropped the Executioner at Klagenfurt, where he picked up a rental car and drove to Graz, roughly seventy miles to the northeast. From there, with first-rate bogus paperwork, it was a simple matter for him to book a flight to Stuttgart. He was forced to wait three hours for the flight to board, which gave him time to think.

If Sestic had been truthful in his final moments—and Bolan had no reason to believe he was lying—then the middleman he dealt with, who accepted the delivery of human "merchandise," was known to spend at least a portion of his time in Stuttgart. That didn't mean that Stuttgart was the center of the slave trade's German link. Bolan knew that the majority of women sold from Bosnia by Sestic and his cronies wound up in the Netherlands, by way of Germany, and that meant active brokers on the job. He had no doubt that one or more German middlemen could point him to the pipeline's architects in Amsterdam.

But he'd have to catch them first.

At least he had a name: Hans Kettering. A check-in with the Stony Man Farm computers, at his secret power base not far from Washington, had come up winners in a hurry. Briefed by long-distance telephone, he'd learned as much about his target of the hour as the FBI, the CIA and Interpol could say.

Hans Kettering was twenty-eight years old, the grandson of a Nazi SS officer who had avoided war crimes prosecution by abandoning the Fatherland in August 1945. He put down roots in Argentina, married and produced four children in the following six years. Rolf was the youngest of the brood, and he returned to Germany when he was ten years old to live with relatives. By that time Rolf had been indoctrinated with his father's master-race philosophy, and when he married, siring children of his own, he passed the lessons on, like some congenital disease.

The product, Hans, was a professional hater. He had logged his first arrest at seventeen, for painting swastikas on headstones at a Jewish cemetery. Other charges followed: battery, attempted arson, vandalism, publication and display of Nazi propaganda. He was idolized by neofascist skinheads and recruited hundreds of them for his street-fighting National Front.

But peddling hate had a limited profit potential, and so young Hans had hired his skinheads out as muscle to the highest bidder, winding up in bed with several ranking mobsters in the former West Germany. Kettering and his commandos had been Johnny-on-the-spot with fists, feet, firebombs—anything it took to rout the competition and ensure a healthy flow of deutsche marks to the proper hands.

From Interpol the word came down that Kettering was under contract for at least the past three years to Gunter Jodl, in Cologne. The forty-two-year-old entrepreneur had earned his first million in the early 1970s, smuggling refugees out of East Berlin for a fee. In later years his name was linked to narcotics traffic, heroin from Turkey, cocaine from Bolivia and shipments of black-market weapons. But the hard core of his operation was commercial sex. He operated at least half a dozen brothels that police were sure of, and took his cut from hookers on the streets—Stuttgart, Mannheim, Berlin and Cologne. German officers had yet to build a case against him that would stand in court.

The Executioner, however, wasn't bound by legal rules of evidence. He had no obligation to prove his case to twelve good people and true beyond a reasonable doubt.

It was a whole new ball game. The stakes were life and death, with no appeals.

Security precautions at the airport had prevented Bolan from traveling armed. He had a contact in Stuttgart who could remedy the hardware shortage, but he felt naked at the moment, knowing it meant trouble if the enemy somehow identified him and had a hit team waiting at the Stuttgart airport.

But Bolan hadn't come this far by letting paranoia rule his life and dictate his movements. Fear could paralyze the strongest warrior if it had free rein, but he preferred to let his adversaries sweat it out, while he kept moving, carrying the battle to their very doorsteps.

He was thumbing through an in-flight magazine when the captain's voice asked everyone to buckle up, as they were seven minutes from their destination. He was followed by a flight attendant speaking English, French and German, offering directions to connecting flights inside the Stuttgart terminal.

He thought about the stand-up comics who complained that "terminal" wasn't the brightest choice of labels for an airport, but it suited Bolan's visit perfectly. How many strangers would be dead before he caught the next flight out?

Enough, perhaps, to slow the heinous traffic.

The Executioner put the magazine away, checked his seat belt and settled back to wait for touchdown.

The war wasn't going to start without him.

HANS KETTERING WAS restless. He paced nervously around the loft that doubled as his home and party headquarters for the National Front. Surrounded by a dozen of his top lieutenants, he rattled off a list of orders, pausing only for the members of his audience to interject acknowledgments of their instructions.

"I want all our people armed," he said, "without exception. Nothing obvious for the police to work on, but we need to be prepared."

"I'm taking care of it," Otto Horst affirmed.

"Not just in Stuttgart," Kettering went on. "We don't know where the enemy may strike."

"Or if there *is* an enemy," Konrad Gelb added.

"Do you think the deaths in Bosnia were accidental?" Kettering demanded.

"The Serbs and Muslims kill each other every day," Gelb said. "There's nothing to suggest our business is involved."

"Would you prefer to wait for a bullet before you take steps to prepare yourself?"

"No, Hans."

"Do you want this Muslim trash invading Germany, as if they owned the Fatherland?"

Gelb shook his head. "No, Hans."

"It is, perhaps, an inconvenience for you to obey my orders?"

Gelb looked weary. "No, Hans."

"What about surveillance at the airports?" Helmut Dankers asked.

"We don't know who we're looking for," Kettering replied. "In Bosnia they executed Sestic and his military sponsor. If Jodl's operations have been singled out, the trail leads back to us."

"We're guarding Jodl, then?" Ulrich Kohl asked.

"Not personally. He has people of his own for that. We take the streets and transport stations, powder labs, the brothels. Nothing obvious, you understand? When the target is revealed, we strike in force and crush them."

"Suppose there are too many of them?" Gelb inquired.

Kettering ceased his pacing and turned to face the young man who seemed bent on challenging his every order. "Are you afraid, Konrad?"

"No." Gelb bristled at the question, as if Kettering had cast aspersions on his manhood.

"Are you not prepared to give your life for the redemption of the Fatherland?"

"I am."

"We're of a single mind, then. There should be no problem."

It seemed to Kettering that Gelb wasn't convinced, but he knew Konrad well enough to trust that he'd do as he was told. If he was forced to press the issue, Kettering had information on a certain hotel fire in Neustadt—three Turks dead and seven injured—that would give him leverage against Gelb.

Or he could just as easily dispose of him with a single phone call.

Kettering hadn't risen to command the National Front by virtue of his charming personality. The post hadn't been vacant when he came along, of course. When Ubel Spangler organized the front in 1987, he'd been more concerned with personal promotion than the future of the Fatherland. There were also rumors that his sexual proclivities were curious, to say the least. A phone call to the police in Darmstadt did the trick. Spangler's second in command was a different proposition, though. It took a bullet in the head to finally remove him from contention.

Kettering had fired the fatal shot himself.

These days, when bloodshed was required, he sent his troops to do the dirty work. The method hadn't failed him yet, and he was reasonably confident it wouldn't fail him now.

If he was wrong, there would be hell to pay, but Kettering wouldn't be picking up the tab. There were inferiors to take the heat.

It was another benefit of standing with the master race.

"IT COULD be trouble."

Willem Ruud didn't sound worried. Instead, his tone was thoughtful, almost introspective, as he sipped his morning coffee. Facing him across a spacious desk, Jani van Zon was clearly ill at ease.

"We should do something, Willem."

"What would you suggest? A trip to Germany, perhaps? Or Bosnia?"

"There must be something," van Zon muttered, but he didn't sound convinced.

"No alerts just yet, but it makes sense for us to prepare ourselves," Ruud replied.

"Is Jodl worried?" van Zon asked.

"He says not, but it would be strange if he wasn't concerned, at least."

"What preparation is he making?"

Ruud could only shrug at that. The Germans tended to keep their feelings to themselves. Still, Ruud understood why deaths in Bosnia wouldn't immediately frighten Jodl and his troops in Germany. The argument that they could always find another source of women inside Bosnia was almost certainly correct, but Ruud disliked the feeling that control was slipping through his fingers, inch by inch, and there was nothing he could do to get it back.

They simply had to wait and see.

If there was any further trouble, logic told him, it would strike at Jodl and the Germans first. Ruud told himself that he could count on ample warning time to put his own troops on the line before the storm broke over him.

Unless . . .

He didn't chase the phantom, knowing it was self-destructive to imagine enemies were none existed. He was six hundred miles from Sarajevo. To seek him out, an enemy not only had to bridge the gap, but also learn Ruud's name, his business, track him down in Amsterdam and penetrate his personal security. Such leaps of logic would require an international conspiracy to give them life. There was no agency on earth possessing such resolve, much less the jurisdiction.

"What are your orders, Willem?"

Van Zon's voice cut through his morbid reverie and brought Ruud back to earth. He frowned, considering exactly how cautious he should be at this early stage, before a threat was even clearly demonstrated.

"Normal supervision of the business," Ruud instructed. "Have the soldiers keep an eye out for suspicious characters, as always, but I don't want anybody going overboard. We don't need paranoia at the moment."

"No." His second in command looked thoughtful. "If something curious should happen . . ."

"You must deal with it, of course. As usual."

"I can't help wondering about the Germans," van Zon said.

"What do you mean?"

"Have you considered that they might have staged this incident themselves?"

"What would their purpose be?" Ruud asked.

"Perhaps they're hoping to consolidate their grip on the supply," van Zon suggested.

"They were doing well enough without a war."

"People get greedy, Willem."

Under different circumstances, Ruud might have smiled, but he wasn't amused this morning. There was cash at stake—and worse—if war broke out among surviving partners in the syndicate. When he considered van Zon's notion, there was just a possibility that he could be correct. But why would a man of Gunter Jodl's standing and experience rock the boat?

Because people got greedy.

No. Ruud caught himself before that train of thought could gather speed. To the best of his knowledge, Jodl had no special contacts in Bosnia. With Sestic and his military backers gone, it meant the Germans would be forced to start all over, forging new connections in the battle-scourged republic. It would mean a greater loss of revenue for Jodl than for Ruud and company, at least in the short run.

"If they control supply," van Zon went on, "they can raise the price at will. We'd have no option but to pay."

"We still have Asian sources," Ruud reminded him.

"True enough, but they have a limited appeal, these days, especially with all the worry about AIDS in the Far East."

"And your solution, Jani, if there *is* a problem?"

"Simple. Anything Jodl and his skinheads can do, we can do better. Find our own connection with the Serbs and cut the Germans out entirely."

"Jodl wouldn't like that," Ruud suggested.

"Just give the word, sir, and I'll get rid of him for you. Kettering, as well."

"I hope it doesn't come to that."

"But if it does, we should be ready. With your permission, I can have a strike team in Cologne by noon. It's just across the border. They can drive and take their weapons with them."

When he thought about it, Ruud couldn't deny that van Zon's plan made sense. If Jodl and his men were innocent of treachery, then it would do no harm to watch them closely for a while. By contrast, if the Germans were conspiring to monopolize the trade and squeeze their partners, it would call for swift reprisals.

If Ruud had been a betting man, he'd have placed his money on some nameless enemy in Bosnia, perhaps a deal gone wrong with Sestic or the officers he bribed to look the other way while he smuggled women from the country. All the same, there were occasions when the likely choice didn't pan out, and it would almost surely be the Germans, if Ruud's first guess didn't hit the mark. In that case it was only wise to be prepared.

"Do you have this team on standby, Jani?"

"Yes, sir."

"All right, then. I suppose it wouldn't hurt to have them take a little drive."

7

Stuttgart traces its name to the middle of the tenth century, when Duke Liutolf established his famous *stutengarten*—literally "stud garden"—for the breeding of Thoroughbred horses. Rebuilt since World War II as one of Germany's leading industrial centers, the home of Porsche, Mercedes-Benz and Zeiss optical equipment, Stuttgart is also a cultural center, famous for its ballet, state opera and philharmonic orchestra. Nor has the city run to type for industrial Meccas, reborn in concrete and steel. Within the city limits, fully two-thirds of the land is devoted to parks, gardens and woodlands.

Bolan entered Stuttgart on a Tuesday afternoon. His first stop from the airport, after picking up a rental car, was a small shop in the suburb of Bad Cannstatt, where he introduced himself to the proprietor, Wilmot Rahn. A part-time contract agent of the CIA, he kept small arms on hand for "special" customers, and Bolan chose a Walther P-1 automatic for his side arm, backing it with an Uzi submachine gun, plus a Steyr AUG assault rifle and 40 mm MECAR rifle grenades. The crowning acquisition of his newfound arsenal was a Walter WA-2000 sniper rifle, chambered for the .300 Winchester Magnum cartridge.

Bolan's next stop was a stylish brothel just off Schillerstrasse, not far from the deluxe Hotel Am Schlossgarten. It was still broad daylight, well short of peak business hours, when he parked the Volkswagen sedan out front. A lightweight raincoat covered the Uzi in a swivel sling beneath his right arm, the Walther P-1 hung beneath his left. The Uzi had a chunky silencer attached, with spare magazines slotted into the raincoat's interior pockets. Any more hardware, Bolan thought, and he'd have clanked as he walked from the curb to the brothel's front door.

He rang the bell and waited until he saw a shadow fall across the peephole from within. He had to have passed scrutiny, for the door opened a moment later to reveal the lady—or the madam—of the house.

"Guten tag, mein Herr."

"Sprechen sie Englisch?" he asked.

"Of course. Come in, mein Herr."

He stepped across the threshold and waited for the door to close behind him. The woman was smiling at him, on the verge of making small talk, when he let her see the submachine gun.

"Gott in himmel!"

"English, please."

"Yes, sir! What is it that you want?"

"How many people are here in the house right now?" he asked.

"Eleven girls and two customers."

"That's all?"

"Except for Kulbert."

"He's muscle?"

"Bitte?"

"House security."

"Yes. Security."

"I want him down here, now."

She nodded, and taking two steps away from Bolan, called to Kulbert, somewhere on the second floor. It took a moment for the gunner to respond—six feet of blond, Teutonic muscle in a shiny suit that bulged beneath one arm. He couldn't be thirty yet, but Bolan recognized the cold eyes of a killer snapping into focus on his SMG.

He was quick, but he couldn't beat the odds as Bolan swung up his Uzi and into target acquisition, squeezing off a short burst from the hip. The parabellum shockers spun Kulbert before he took an awkward header down the stairs.

The madam gave a little squeal of shock and was about to bolt, when Bolan caught her by the arm and held her fast.

"You're shutting down," he told her, leaning close and making sure she followed every word. "I want the women out of here inside five minutes, understand?"

"I don't... Where should we go?"

"It doesn't matter where. Whoever sticks around is getting scorched."

Bolan left her to it. He stalked through the well-appointed parlor to the kitchen. They used gas, as he'd hoped. It was a moment's work to snuff the pilot light and turn the burners on full-blast. He'd noticed candelabrum standing on the polished dining table, and he took it into the kitchen. Setting it beside the sink, he lighted all three candles, then retreated from the room.

The madam had her charges on the move when Bolan got back to the parlor, including two men in their middle forties dressing on the run.

The joy house refugees were sprinting down the street, and Bolan had his car in motion when the candles did their job. There was a flash and thunderclap behind him, as a fireball filled his rearview mirror.

One down.

HARVEY RITTER TOOK a last drag on his cigarette and stubbed the butt into an ashtray fashioned from the sawed-off base of an 88 mm artillery shell. It pleased him to imagine that shell, and ten thousand like it, being fired against the Allied troops on D-Day.

His reflection in the full-length mirror brought a smile to his face. His cap fit snugly against his close-cropped scalp, a silver death's head glaring from above the plastic visor. On the collar of his jet-black tunic, silver lightning bolts proclaimed his admiration of the great SS, which came so close to purifying Europe and the world at large. He admired the way his riding breeches hugged his thighs and calves, while flaring like a cobra's hood around the hips. His jack boots had been polished to a mirror shine. The pistol on his hip, supported by a wide black belt, was a classic Luger P-08, first issued in the closing days of World War II, preserved and cherished by three generations of his family.

The armband Ritter wore wasn't the standard issue for his party. German law forbade display of swastikas, and the National Front therefore took as its emblem a rough facsimile, three lightning bolts exploding from a central hub. For Ritter the pale imitation left much to be desired. In his private moments he preferred to strip the armband off and wear the real thing in its place.

Like now.

Downstairs, his boys were drinking beer and getting rowdy, talking up their latest skirmishes against the Turks and Pakistanis. Some of them had minor cuts and bruises, but all the really hard knocks had been suffered by the other side.

As it should always be.

The raids weren't all race and politics, of course. The new Reich needed money, just like any other government-to-be, and Kettering had arranged for contracts with selected German businessmen who needed muscle now and then.

It didn't trouble Ritter when the Front commanded him to field his troops in the defense of pimps and gangsters. Prostitution was, in Ritter's view, a valuable public service. Properly administered and taxed, the flesh trade could minimize domestic tension, sex crimes and degeneracy in a civilized society. National socialism placed no moral stigma on prostitutes or their keepers.

The house on Sophienstrasse had been taken over by the Front eleven months before, and remodeled slightly to accommodate a dozen soldiers sleeping over at a time. So far, there had been no conflict with the neighbors, who were mostly solid Aryans. The skinheads were relatively quiet, and their presence in the neighborhood had reduced the local crime rate by an estimated eighty-two percent.

Ritter was about to go downstairs and get himself a beer, when an explosion rocked the floor beneath his feet. He staggered but didn't fall. He whipped his Luger from its holster and raced toward the door.

By the time he reached the stairs, he could smell smoke, and then the sound of gunfire reached his ears. The staccato bursts sounded like an automatic rifle, ripping wood and plaster, echoing in screams. He flicked off the Luger's safety and clenched the pistol tightly enough to make his knuckles blanche.

One of his soldiers—it was hard to tell which one with all that blood smeared on his face—lurched toward the stairs and toppled forward, blocking Ritter's path. Ritter vaulted over the body and kept on going into the parlor, which now resembled a slaughterhouse.

The one man left standing was a stranger to Ritter. The rifle in his hands could only be the Steyr AUG, an unmistakable configuration with its magazine behind the pistol grip, factory standard optical sight and grenade launcher. Ritter had fired such a weapon on training exercises, and he knew that one of the MECAR grenades could account for the gaping hole where the front door used to be.

But this was no time to think about the man's identity, who'd sent him or what he wanted. He was an enemy, and he had to die.

The Luger seemed to weigh a ton. Ritter used both hands to brace it, sighting on the tall man's chest. His finger curled around the trigger, taking up the slack.

He saw flame sputter from the muzzle of the AUG, felt something like a giant fist slam hard against his rib cage. The impact pitched Ritter backward, off his feet. He knew the wet warmth soaking through his shirt and slacks could only be blood.

The stranger stood above him. There was no anger in his face, no evidence that he felt anything at all. Before the image faded out forever, it occurred to Ritter that his killer was the perfect warrior, an emotionless assassin.

He would have made a valiant Aryan.

FIFTY MILES NORTHWEST of Stuttgart, Mannheim stands at the convergence of the Neckar and the Rhine rivers. The city is constructed on a gridiron pattern dating from the 1600s, with the north-south streets labeled from A on the west to U on the east, while east-west streets are numbered from the center outward, heading north or south. Thus, if a newcomer is told that his hotel's address is C-2, he should expect to find it three blocks inland from the Rhine and two blocks north of downtown Mannheim.

Bolan kept the grid in mind as he looked for the first of several targets he had marked in Mannheim. Situated in the block that was dubbed A-6, he found a warehouse fronting on the Rhine. Most days, the merchandise it held was standard—large appliances, machinery, consumer goods—but once a month, on average, the warehouse was converted to a dormitory under guard, where women smuggled into Germany illegally were held, pending their assignment to domestic brothels or export to foreign markets. If the information gleaned from Interpol was accurate, at least a hundred women made the one-way trip each year, from Thailand, the Philippines, Argentina and from Bosnia-Herzegovina.

There were no guards visible outside the warehouse as Bolan parked the rental car and made his choice of weapons, going with the silencer-equipped Uzi and a handful of incendiary sticks.

He locked the car and walked to the warehouse through a drizzling rain. His hair was plastered to his scalp before he reached the loading dock and tried the door he found there. It was locked, and Bolan spent a moment with his picks to get it open, careful not to make a sound that would alert the enemy. When he was safe across the threshold, Bolan brought his Uzi out from under cover.

Moving past a smallish, glassed-in office, then down a narrow corridor, he followed distant voices to the main floor of the warehouse. Two men stood beside a yellow forklift, killing time. They were unarmed, and Bolan saw no need to kill them if they didn't force his hand. Instead, he cleared his throat and let them see the Uzi, stepping closer when they raised their hands.

It had worked once before, and he tried it again: "*Sprechen sie Englisch?*"

The shorter of the two answered. "I speak some English."

"Good. You're leaving now, before this place goes up in smoke." He registered the man's relief. "I have a message for your boss, though."

"Yes?"

"He needs to know it isn't healthy to work for a man like Gunter Jodl. This is payback, and I'm only getting started. Do you understand?"

"The words, I understand. Herr Jodl I do not know."

"That's fine. Just tell your boss exactly what I said."

He punctuated his instructions with the Uzi, waggling its heavy muzzle in the general direction of the door. The man nodded once and took off running, with his colleague close behind.

When they were gone, Bolan took a seat behind the forklift's steering wheel and turned the key to get it started. He shifted into gear and goosed the pedal just enough to start the vehicle rolling on a slow collision course with what appeared to be a stack of crated freezers or household refrigerators. Stepping down nimbly, he fired a short burst to drill the fuel tank, laying down a liquid trail as the forklift proceeded on its way.

He then palmed a slim incendiary stick and primed it with a twist. He dropped it in the forklift's wake, retreating as it sizzled, sparked and caught the trail of gasoline. Flames ran along the floor like magic, overtaking the forklift.

By the time the tank exploded, Bolan was retreating through the outer corridor and past the vacant office, out across the loading dock and back through the drizzle to his car.

He didn't wait around to see the warehouse burning in the rain. The war was moving on.

HARDY FINSTER POURED a cup of coffee from his Thermos bottle, set the cap on the dashboard of his ancient Porsche and capped the bottle before wedging it between the seats. Beside him Alvin Breit was chewing gum and smoking, keeping one hand tucked inside his jacket, wrapped around the handle of his gun.

For all Finster knew, it was another false alarm. They were forever being warned of imminent attacks by enemies who never arrived, and Finster told himself that this was probably another futile exercise, occasioned by the paranoia of the men who paid the bills.

Finster merely followed orders, whether it required vandalizing establishments, assaulting undesirables, or, as was the case now, standing watch outside a whorehouse in Mannheim. It was all the same to him. His satisfaction came from knowing he had done the best job he could. He was a soldier, nothing more.

"Hell, this is boring," Breit said, chewing gum as he spoke. It made a smacking sound, setting Finster's nerves on edge.

"It's not supposed to be exciting. It's a job, not entertainment."

"I could use some action, even so." Breit leered. "If we're supposed to watch a whorehouse, we could do it just as well from the inside."

"We have our orders. Make the best of it," Finster said.

"That's what I mean. We should be inside to make the best of it," Breit insisted.

There seemed to be no point in answering. Finster took another sip of coffee and stared at the house across the street.

"What's going on?" he blurted as the front door opened to disgorge a rush of six or seven women, mostly clad in robes and underwear. There was a muffled popping sound, like fireworks, gone almost before it registered. The next thing Finster knew, a thread of smoke wafted through the open door, growing thicker by the second.

"Gunshots! Come on! The house is burning!"

Finster slammed the driver's door behind him and raced across the street with Breit close on his heels, the SIG-Sauer automatic leaping to his hand. He wasted no time questioning the whores. They were disoriented, frightened. Whatever lay behind that fear was still inside the burning house.

Without a handkerchief to mask his mouth and nose, Finster raised his left arm as a partial screen against the smoke. His eyes were smarting by the time he'd taken three steps across the threshold, sweeping with the automatic as he tried to scan for targets. Breit jostled him, and Finster lashed out with his free hand, cursing.

In front of him a human shape emerged from the drifting smoke, confronting Finster from a range of six or seven feet. He had some kind of automatic weapon in his hands, and he held it tight against his hip, the muzzle aimed at Finster's chest.

Finster had a bulletproof vest back in his room that would have saved his life—if only he was wearing it. You didn't put the armor on for milk runs, though, and he was left with no recourse except to try to kill the stranger before he had a chance to fire.

The Uzi whispered, spitting death, and Finster felt the parabellum bullets ripping into him, slamming him against the wall. He lost his automatic as he hit the floor, and his hands clutched at his wounded abdomen.

Breit got off two shots in rapid fire before the Uzi spoke again, and he went down, legs thrashing in the smoke.

The stranger came to stand in front of Finster, kicking the SIG-Sauer out of reach.

"It's nothing personal," he said in English, then turned and walked away.

Finster thought briefly that his employer would give him hell when he learned that he hadn't taken out the stranger who hit the whorehouse. He closed his eyes, and suddenly it didn't matter anymore.

8

Josef Pries, a veteran security officer of the Bundespolizei in Bonn, had seen his share of action in the dirty war against terrorists of the left and right—or red and black, as they preferred to call themselves. In his twelve years on the force, he had contended with fanatics from the Red Army Faction, the Gray Wolves, Black June—a whole rainbow of killers, in fact. Along the way he'd been shot three times, and he'd killed five terrorists, including a young woman.

He'd never worked the vice beat until now. If anything, he shared some measure of his fellow officers' derision for the "prostie cops" who spent their hours chasing pimps, pornographers and whores. From what he'd been told, this job was different, though.

It had to do with neo-Nazi skinheads, high on Pries's hit list for the past three years. There had been rumbles that the skins were hiring out as sluggers for a number of the wealthy German pimps and pushers, but Pries was more concerned with their political activities and violations of the law proscribing Naziism.

Now, judging from the sketchy information he'd been given, the two concerns were overlapping. The chat with his immediate superior had seemed deliberately vague, in Pries's estimation. It had the smell of "plausible deniability" about it, meaning he'd be on the hook, alone, if anything went wrong. He was accustomed to the method—often used when he was working undercover and the brass suspected he'd have to break some laws while building up his cover—but the new assignment had a couple of unique, suspicious twists.

First, he'd be working with a foreigner, an American, which was a first for Pries. His captain had told him the American was "someone special," but he either didn't know or wouldn't say which agency Mike Belasko represented.

Furthermore, it was the first assignment he'd faced without a briefing on the prospect of arrests and prosecutions. Quite the opposite, in fact. His captain had made it clear that the courts and Pries's fellow officers weren't to be involved.

It was to be a hunting expedition, apparently, and while the notion had occurred to Pries, it never crossed his mind that he'd ever truly be unleashed to stalk his enemies.

Pries wondered briefly if it was some kind of trap. Lord knew he had his share of enemies, both on and off the force. His gruff, uncompromising view of law and order often terrified ambitious, career-driven officers, and several of them had surpassed him in promotion during recent years.

He told himself that he was getting paranoid, an occupational hazard for policemen in general, and undercover agents in particular. He'd find out what this Belasko wanted from him, and then decide if it was worth the risk.

He'd picked the Alter Zoll, an ancient fortress overlooking the Rhine, as the location for his rendezvous with the American. Pries had a fair description of the man, and was advised that he'd have a copy of the latest *Newsweek* magazine—the international edition—folded underneath his arm. It should be relatively safe, but he wanted time to check the meeting site and satisfy himself that he wasn't about to put his head inside a noose.

Pries had lived through ambushes before. The last one, sixteen months earlier, had nearly killed him. He'd lost four pints of blood, a portion of his liver and a month of work while he recuperated from his wounds. The incident hadn't broken his nerve, but he was certainly more cautious now.

The Alter Zoll drew tourists like a magnet, with its mix of history and scenery. A lovely promenade extended from the fortress, following the Rhine to the former Bundeshaus, or German federal parliament. This evening Pries picked out a dozen couples, three with children, and as many solo tourists wandering around the parapets and grounds. None of them matched Belasko's physical description, but there were still fifteen minutes left before the rendezvous.

Reaching underneath his sport coat, Pries adjusted the holster on his hip, drawing reassurance from the Browning double-action automatic.

BOLAN THOUGHT HE HAD to have set some kind of record for the drive from Mannheim into Bonn. The German autobahns were spacious and well maintained, and everyone seemed to drive as if they had their hearts set on the pole position at the Indy 500. Bolan put the hundred miles behind him in an hour and seven minutes, flat.

He had no difficulty following the posted signs until he reached the Alter Zoll. Night was coming on, and there was ample room for Bolan's rental in the parking lot. He locked it, and, just in case, took the Uzi with him, dangling underneath his raincoat on the leather swivel rig.

He didn't know his contact and had no physical description of the officer who would, presumably, be waiting for him somewhere in the fortress. The recognition signal, folded underneath his arm, had been the last copy available at the newsstand, three blocks from the Alter Zoll. The cover screamed about atrocities in Africa, but that was hardly news by now.

Names and faces changed, but it seemed to Bolan that the suffering was all the same. With any luck the information he obtained this night would help him ease that suffering for some and bring a little justice home to those responsible.

He walked around the fortress grounds without direction. It was the contact's job to seek him out and make the approach.

"It's good to keep abreast of world events."

A man's voice, speaking English, came from his blind side. Bolan turned to face a stranger in his thirties, wearing nondescript civilian clothes.

"Of course, you can't trust everything you read," he answered, finishing the prearranged signal.

"Mike Belasko?"

"In the flesh."

"I'm Josef Pries." The hand that shook Bolan's had a firm, dry grip. "Let's take a walk."

The tourist ranks were thinning, and soon the beer halls would be warming up.

"You're after Gunter Jodl and his skinhead playmates," Pries said to get things rolling.

"That's the rumor."

"I wasn't aware Herr Jodl dealt with the United States."

"I'm hoping he'll never get the chance."

"Preventive medicine, I think you call it?" There was something like wry amusement in Pries's voice.

"More or less."

"You have just arrived in Germany?"

Bolan thought about dodging the question, then decided to play it straight. He needed full cooperation from his contact, and starting with a lie seemed like a shaky way to go.

"I spent some time down south. In Stuttgart and Mannheim."

"Ah."

It stood to reason that Pries would know about the violence in those cities. Rumbles, anyway, if he'd been assigned to work with Bolan.

"What is it you require from me?" Pries asked.

"You had a briefing?"

"It was, how shall I say, deliberately vague," Pries said with a smile.

Bolan got the message. Headquarters had given him a blanket order to cooperate, but brass hats were survivors: they avoided any detailed orders that could rebound to their disadvantage down the line.

"This Jodl character is bringing women out of Bosnia and Third World countries, and selling them in Amsterdam. I have the go-ahead to shut the operation down by any means required," the Executioner said.

Pries was silent for a moment. "Then I'm aware of Jodl's business, though I don't work vice. He uses Nazi skinheads to protect his network."

"That's the word."

When Pries spoke next, his voice was thoughtful. "We have a weakness, my fellow countrymen and I. Most of us crave an orderly existence—civilized, productive, technological, affluent. In pursuit of those ideals, we trust authority, sometimes too much. My father's generation took a madman to their hearts because he offered them a 'final solution' to all their problems. We have suffered for that choice, but there's still a part of Germany, in all of us, that wants to hear a rousing march and join the great parade."

"That's history," Bolan said. "Decent men can always change the future."

"I believe this, too—on some days more than others. It's why I've spent the past twelve years opposing terrorism. Now, it would appear, you want me to become a terrorist."

"Not quite. The men I'm hunting are the terrorists. When you take a stand against their kind, I call it self-defense."

"I find it difficult to justify employing tactics they, themselves, would use," Pries replied.

"If it helps," Bolan said, "I'm mostly seeking information. Names, addresses. Targets. You don't have to help me take them down. In fact—"

Pries raised a hand to interrupt. "When I was twenty-eight," he said, "I shot and killed a nineteen-year-old girl. She was a terrorist with seven murders to her credit, and she tried to make me number eight before I put her down. I tell you this so you'll know I'm not afraid of dirty hands.

"If I decide to help you," he went on, "I will not be relegated to the sidelines. But you have to understand there will be no support from the police. In fact they might try to arrest us both."

"Okay."

"You've done this kind of thing before, I think."

"A time or two," the Executioner admitted.

"I sense that. May I ask a question?"

"Fire away."

"How do you sleep?"

"With one eye open," Bolan said, "assuming I can find the time."

"And are there faces in your dreams?"

"Sometimes."

"How do you make them go away?"

"If they ever do, then I'll tell you."

Pries thought about his answer for a moment.

"Let's discuss your plan," he said at last.

WHEN THEY WERE FINISHED and had separated for the moment, Josef Pries had time to think about the course of action he'd chosen for himself. It would be dangerous, of course; that much was understood. The risk wasn't entirely physical, however. For him there was another level of responsibility that he couldn't overlook: the matter of his conscience.

The choice was ultimately his, which way to go, and he'd chosen to cooperate with Mike Belasko.

There was something in the American's manner that made Pries trust him . . . to a point. The man was still a stranger, but Pries was adept at sizing up people without a lot of background information to assist him. Working undercover as he often did, it was a critical survival skill.

Belasko was a warrior. There was a look about him, something in the eyes, the way he carried himself, that told Pries the man had been tested in battle, not once but many times. The fact that he was still alive bore testimony to his skill, if not his motives.

Yet, Belasko's method gave him pause. He wondered whether he could do it, when the chips were down...and whether he could live with it when he was done.

One problem at a time, Pries told himself. There was no guarantee he'd survive the next few hours, and a dead man had no worries.

The morbid thought brought a small, unbidden smile to Pries's face. He knew his chosen course was risky when he started taking consolation from the fact that he might not survive to feel the heat when it was done. Of course if Belasko's plan worked, there'd be no reports to file, no evidence for his superiors to grumble over, looking for a scapegoat.

Pries thought about the killing, what it had to feel like to stalk a man with no intention of taking him alive. But in his opinion, the skinheads were nothing more than a gang of rabid animals, exulting in their reputation for explosive, random violence. Now, on top of hate crimes, they were hiring out as mercenaries to scum like Gunter Jodl, cashing in on human misery. They would be no great loss.

As for Jodl and his cronies, Pries didn't care that they ran prostitutes, per se. If men and women sold their bodies voluntarily, without coercion, it was no concern of his. Slave trading was a totally different proposition.

By any reckoning, the man was garbage. He and Belasko would be taking out the trash.

Pries understood that he was rationalizing his decision. But if he could make a dent in evil by exerting some strategic force, it would be worth the pain his conscience suffered as a result.

And he'd learn to live with it, as Mike Belasko had.

Cologne is big on culture, big on industry, and big on tourism. It's also big on vice, and served as the headquarters for the syndicate established and controlled by Gunter Jodl.

Bolan's first stop in Cologne, near midnight, was a cut-rate joy house on a street named Putz. The irony was too delicious to ignore, and if it felt like starting small, he knew there'd be ample targets in the city before he brought the curtain down. With Pries on board, they had a chance to double up and cover twice the ground in half the time.

The drizzling rain had passed by the time Bolan parked his rental car and locked it. Scudding clouds and garish city lights obscured the stars above. They were up there, somewhere, just as Bolan knew his enemies were waiting for him somewhere in the city.

That was his advantage. After the preliminary rounds, the Grim Reaper was closing in on Gunter Jodl, and the slaver didn't even know it yet.

He wore the Uzi with its silencer beneath his raincoat, the pockets weighted with a smoke grenade and extra magazines. The Walther P-1 automatic was snugged in its shoulder rig. There was no way of telling if the brothel would be guarded, but the events in

Stuttgart and Mannheim would have put his enemies on guard.

The place was jumping when he got there. There was a topless club to get the johns warmed up before they made their picks and went upstairs. Two women, a blonde and redhead, were on stage when Bolan paid his cover charge and entered the smoky darkness, heavy metal music screaming from strategic speakers situated at the four points of the compass, covering all quarters of the room.

A hostess met him just across the threshold, took his hand and led him to a table, where she settled in beside him, close enough for Bolan to enjoy her cleavage from a bird's-eye view. She had her right hand on his thigh before the waitress arrived to take the standard order for a pair of watered drinks at twice the normal charge. Before the liquor came, she had her hands full, stroking Bolan, getting down to business.

"You enjoy the show?" she asked him.

"I'm beginning to."

"You think I'm pretty?"

"Absolutely."

"We could go upstairs," she said. "I have a room."

It was the ticket he was waiting for, and Bolan didn't quibble over price. "Let's go," he said.

Bolan let her take his hand, and they made their way upstairs, past a hardman in a tux. The bouncer flicked a glance at Bolan as they passed, but nothing seemed to register behind the brooding eyes.

The second floor was lined with numbered doors, fourteen in all, and Bolan's hostess led him to the second on the left. The room held only a smallish bed, one straight-backed chair and a closet with the door removed.

She was about to help him lose his raincoat, when he brought out the Uzi and pressed a finger to her lips, her warning cry contained before she had a chance to let it rip.

"Be quiet and you won't get hurt," he told her. "Understand?"

She nodded, wide-eyed, and made no sound as Bolan took his hand away.

"I'm looking for the manager. The boss."

"Herr Ludke," she replied breathlessly.

"Close enough. Where is he?"

"He has an office, up." She pointed toward the ceiling, indicating the third floor.

"Okay, I'm leaving now. But we don't want anybody thinking you cooperated, do we?"

Her translation lagged a beat or two, her eyes wide and staring at the Uzi. "Nein," she whispered.

"So, turn around."

Bolan pulled the punch and barely tapped her skull behind one ear. It was enough to leave a knotty bruise and render her unconscious. He left her stretched out on the narrow bed and went to find Herr Ludke on the floor above.

Another sentry was posted on the third floor, and he reached for his gun when he saw the SMG in Bolan's hand. The Uzi stuttered, pinned him to the wall with hollowpoints before his bulk gave in to gravity and settled to the floor, a crimson smear on the plaster following his progress.

The office door was labeled *PRIVAT*, and Bolan kicked it in. He caught a fat, bald man rising from behind a spacious desk. He was about to snarl a question when he saw Bolan's submachine gun pointed at his face. His right hand darted for the desk drawer, but before he could grab the pistol hidden there, Bolan nailed him with a short burst to the chest that slammed him backward over the padded swivel chair. Ludke sounded like a redwood falling, but his death wouldn't be heard in the noisy club downstairs.

Retreating to the second floor, the Executioner palmed the smoke grenade, released its safety pin and dropped the bomb in the middle of the hallway. He left it hissing, spewing fumes to rout the couples from their bedrooms as he made his way downstairs.

The guard for the second floor was surprised to see Bolan back so soon. His leer disappeared when Bolan told him, "You should have a look around upstairs. It smells like something's burning."

"Bitte?"

"Skip it."

Bolan was on the sidewalk by the time alarm bells started to clamor, and customers spilled out behind him in their rush to the street.

Fire sale, he thought, and smiled.

It was the end of the beginning in Cologne. Perhaps, for Gunter Jodl, it was the beginning of the end.

THE DRIVE FROM BONN to Cologne had taken half an hour in separate cars. Pries had a list of targets, and he started at the top, with a beer hall frequented by Hans Kettering's skinheads. The alley in back was dark and foul-smelling, but it gave him room to park his car and go in through the back door of the club.

Pries wore the Browning double-action automatic on his hip in a pancake holster, but his main pick for the outing was a Heckler & Koch submachine gun, the MP-5 SD-3 model with a built-on silencer and telescoping stock. He clutched the weapon beneath his left arm, for a cross-hand draw. As he moved along the alley, his trench coat flapping around him like a cape, he felt both excited and frightened. But an icy calm had set in by the time he reached for the doorknob, felt it turn and made his way inside.

The storeroom smelled of smoke and stale beer. The door to the main room of the beer hall had a porthole in it, the smudged glass giving Pries a blurred, somewhat distorted view of the interior. He counted fifteen skinheads in his field of vision, five of them young women, but he knew there could be others to his left or right. And how many of them would be packing guns?

He dipped into the right-hand pocket of his raincoat and lifted out the stun grenade that he'd brought along to give himself an edge. He dropped the safety pin, made sure the MP-5 SD-3's safety was off and the fire selector set for 3-round bursts, before using his knee to nudge the door ajar. A low, underhanded pitch set the canister rolling across the floor of the club. Then he stepped back from the doorway, closed his eyes and waited for the thunder.

The blast was somewhat muffled by the intervening door and wall. He went in on the heels of the explosion, tracking with the SMG.

Behind the bar, a chunky older man was on his knees, his hands held against his ears. His meaty arms were mottled with tattoos, a skinhead trademark, and a sawed-off shotgun lay within his reach, suspended from a hook above the register. Pries took no chances and shot him in the chest with three rounds from a range of six or seven feet. The dead man toppled over backward, gasping in surprise.

Pries stepped around the bar and met a younger skinhead struggling to his feet. Although blinded from the flash of the grenade and stunned by its concussion, he still had the strength to grope beneath his leather jacket for the pistol tucked inside his waistband. Three parabellum shockers lifted him completely off his feet and dropped him in his tracks, the handgun spinning out of reach as lifeless fingers lost their purchase.

Pries moved on.

Two skinheads, a male and a female, crouched behind an overturned table, sloshing in a pool of beer. Pries shot the man and stopped the woman's stream of curses with a buttstroke from his SMG.

So much for chivalry.

Pries counted half a dozen skinheads he hadn't seen before and realized that he'd used nine of his thirty rounds to kill three men. He carried extra magazines, of course, but precious time would be lost in reloading, so he thumbed the switch to semiauto fire, for single shots.

Next up was a bear in human form who had to have weighed at least 230 pounds, his belly straining denim jeans and a leather jacket. Pries sighted on the man's forehead and plugged a round between his eyes. He'd already turned in search of other prey before the corpse had toppled forward.

A pistol cracked behind him, drawing his attention. The shot was high and wide, but the punk was soon lining up another, squinting over open gunsights, cursing the blurring effects of the stun grenade. Pries fired twice to take him down, a chest wound and a head shot, slamming him against the bar with lethal force.

The killings ran together after that. Pries worked his way around the room, dispatching first one man and then another. When the magazine was empty, he reloaded, trailing spent brass in his wake. Before he finished, several of the skinheads were on their feet, still disoriented, but with sense enough to try to either fight or get out.

One bruiser came at Pries with a chair, lips drawn back from his teeth in a snarl. The cop shot him in the face and let momentum do the rest, deadweight colliding with the bar and buckling to the cartridge-littered floor. A younger, thinner skinhead drew a boot knife and prepared to throw it overhand, but Pries didn't give him time. A quick 9 mm double-tap went in on target.

The floor was slick with blood as he completed his circuit of the room. The female members were huddled in a corner, cursing him in terms that would have made a sailor blush. It crossed his mind to finish them and spare himself the risk of witnesses, but Pries couldn't bring himself to fire on women when they posed no threat beyond the verbal, offered no resistance and appeared to be unarmed.

The skinhead code of silence would prevent their talking to police, and he reckoned circumstance would do the rest. They were confused, still dazed from the explosion, terrified by the proximity of sudden death.

He left the same way he'd entered, feeling almost giddy from the rush of combat. Seated once more in his car, Pries found his hands were trembling, and he clutched the steering wheel as if to hide the tremor from himself.

He was across the line now, all the way. This night's work constituted murder—and mass murder, at that.

Yet those he'd killed were terrorists who boasted of their crimes against humanity and sang the praises of a dark regime. If killers were eliminated regardless of the means, surely it followed that society was better off?

He was in the game, and there was no way he could call time-out while he went looking for his nerve. It was enough, perhaps, for him to think about the would-be victims he'd saved by weeding out prospective murderers.

Pries hoped so, anyway.

THE LOCK BOX WAS an old apartment house on Dreikonigen Strasse, near the riverfront. Most passersby would hardly spare a second glance for the weathered brick and woodwork, not quite shabby, but within six months or so of needing paint. The renovation, two years earlier, had all gone down inside, with most of it devoted to insuring privacy. The place was soundproof, for a start; you could have fired a cannon in the living room without disturbing the next-door neighbors. Within the house the several rooms were also insulated, so that customers wouldn't disturb one another when their little games got out of hand.

Lock boxes catered to a "special" clientele. Privacy was guaranteed by the proprietor but only for a hefty price. The clientele, therefore, ran more to bankers, lawyers, doctors and the like.

Nobody gets inside a lock box uninvited. There were codes and passwords, often private escorts to ensure the clientele was "clean." No tails, no guns, no badges. Any tools or weapons needed by the john to make his dreams come true were thoughtfully provided by the management. If cops came knocking, there were often tunnels, secret exits or, at least, a working cleanup plan that would eliminate potential witnesses. In the event an undercover officer should somehow make his way inside, he could be made to disappear without a trace.

It would have taken weeks for Bolan to arrange an introduction, buy himself entrance to the lock box, and he didn't have the time to spare. Instead, he went in through the apartment building next door and walked up the ten flights to the roof. The lock box was one story shorter, and he had an easy drop of fifteen feet to reach the service door. As luck would have it, there was no lookout on the roof.

The property and all within belonged to Gunter Jodl. He wouldn't be on the premises, of course, and that was fine. His time was coming. Bolan meant to deal with first things first.

The double locks were new but nothing fancy. Bolan beat them with his picks in ninety seconds flat, then gave the doorknob a twist and a shove. It didn't give; there had to be a bolt on the inside. He decided he'd have to take a chance, banking on the fact that the place was insulated.

He took a step back from the door, raised his silenced Uzi and fired four rounds on semiauto. When he tried the door again, it offered no resistance.

Bolan waited on the threshold for another moment, staring into darkness, listening for any sound that would suggest an armed response. When he was satisfied, he cautiously descended to the topmost floor and started checking out apartments, eight in all. The doors didn't lock automatically, but rather waited for a key. Since none of the eight rooms was occupied at present, they were all unlocked.

Five minutes later he'd reached the third floor. This time one of the doors was locked when Bolan tried it. Relying on the enemy's security precautions to protect him, Bolan kicked in the door and found a youth of sixteen or seventeen pinned with duct tape to a heavy straight-backed chair. The man who knelt in front of him was somewhere in his thirties.

Bolan let the butt of his Uzi do the talking for him, delivering a blow to the man's head that had him flat on the floor. He stepped over the prostrate body, then used a folding knife to free the youth from his bonds.

"Stay here," he said in fractured German. "The police are coming."

Whether Bolan got it wrong, or there was something in the nature of the youth that made him frightened of police, he never knew. The kid was up and running in a flash, past Bolan, out the door and down the hallway to the stairs. Twenty feet behind him, Bolan hit the stairs just as the boy collided with a couple of guards on the second floor.

One of the goons was grappling with the youth, his partner hauling out an automatic pistol, when they both saw Bolan on the stairs. The warrior shot the armed guard first, the Uzi stuttering, and dropped him where he stood. Before he hit the ground, the dying man squeezed off a shot that pierced the door immediately to his right.

And that left one.

The slugger needed both hands to control the squirming teen and lift him up to form a human shield. He spoke, and Bolan didn't need a Berlitz course to figure out what he was saying: Keep your distance, or I'll hurt the boy.

Negotiation was impossible, and Bolan didn't even care to try. His first shot missed the youth's head by inches, opened up the slugger's cheek and sent both figures sprawling to the carpet. The kid was gone before his erstwile captor had struggled to his knees, blood streaming from his lacerated face. The next shot found its mark and the hardman vaulted over backward, dead before he hit the floor.

On Bolan's left the bullet-punctured door swung open to reveal a swarthy face. The man sized up the situation and tried to slam the door, but he was tardy off the mark. Bolan got there with a flying kick that drove him backward to land unconscious on the floor.

His selection from the lock-box menu was an adolescent female, tied across a padded wooden sawhorse. Her thighs and buttocks were a crazy quilt of bruises.

Bolan took a moment with his knife to free the girl. She too, was unconscious, and he placed her in the corridor, as far as possible from her tormentor, then sorted through the man's clothes until he found a jacket that would cover her.

The other rooms were empty. There was no one on the ground floor, where a heavy insulated door stood open to the street. There was also no sign of the youth when Bolan poked his head outside. It was clearly time to go.

He jogged back to his car and drove four blocks before he found a public telephone and got through to the police. He gave the lock-box address twice before he cradled the receiver.

Back inside the car and driving toward his rendezvous with Josef Pries, Bolan wished the little kid well.

God willing, he'd find some help and comfort in the long, dark night.

The man who'd staged his nightmare was about to learn that there was no safe haven from the Executioner.

Gunter Jodl's walled estate lay on the southern outskirts of Cologne. He was rich enough—and free enough with bribes to the authorities—that no one questioned where he got the money for the house and grounds, the limousine, chauffeur and bodyguards.

The last time Josef Pries had been this nervous, he was still a rookie on the force, about to make his first arrest. That night had been a milestone in his life, and so was this. Already far outside the law, he was about to stage an armed assault against the most influential pimp in Germany. With only Mike Belasko on his side, they were outnumbered nine or ten to one. Those were long odds, and if anything went wrong, they'd be on their own.

The wall was eight feet high, with razor wire on top, but Pries wore heavy boots and padded leather gloves to protect him.

On the other side three Dobermans, as sleek as guided missiles, rushed toward him through the early-morning darkness. They were silent, not a bark among them, and Pries wondered if it came from training or the kind of surgery that severed vocal cords. There was no time to challenge either theory, and he shot them with his submachine gun as they charged him, a silent death for silent guardians.

He took a moment to deposit their corpses underneath a sculpted topiary hedge before moving in the direction of the house. A few lights burned on the ground floor.

Pries met his first two-legged sentry fifty yards on, a husky man with close-cropped hair who had a riot shotgun tucked beneath his arm. Pries fired, and the man toppled forward, sprawling onto the grass without a sound. He left the shotgun where it was, wedged underneath the body, and moved on.

He almost tripped over the second gunman, triggered three rounds from the hip in reflex action, hoping that he'd be fast enough to drop the man before his own gun spoke. But this watcher also had a shotgun, and as he fell, the weapon blew a crater in the grass between his feet.

So much for stealth.

Pries cursed and started toward the house, afraid he might already be too late.

IT WAS A SHOCK to any man of wealth and power when the feeling of security he took for granted was abruptly stripped away. The first reaction, normally, was rage at the impertinence of those who would defy him. When the rage brought no result, then doubt set in, and fear was never far behind. Thus Gunter Jodl began to understand that he wasn't invincible.

Hans Kettering sat with him, in the library of Jodl's stylish home, and tried to bring his boss around with promises of bloody vengeance once their adversaries were identified. Of course, that was the problem. After lightning raids in Stuttgart, Mannheim and Cologne, they still had no idea whom they were dealing with or what the series of attacks was designed to accomplish.

Kettering had blamed the Serbs at first, some kind of plot to leapfrog over Jodl's net and deal directly with the buyers out of Amsterdam, but he had scrapped that theory hours earlier. Descriptions of the gunmen—even as fragmentary as they were—suggested two men of a rather different type.

"How are they doing this?" Jodl asked, breaking the silence.

Kettering could no more answer that now than he could the first time he was asked, but he had a new suggestion.

"Suppose they were connected to the law, somehow," he said. "Like vigilantes, or the death squads down in South America."

The look on Jodl's face spoke volumes. "Death squads? South America? You think we're dealing with some maniac from Argentina or Brazil?"

"Something *like* the death squads, maybe. Have you thought about GSG-9?"

"They don't concern themselves with vice," Jodl said. "They're political."

"I know that. But suppose you weren't the target. If they were after the National Front—"

"Then there would be no point in disturbing my business," Jodl retorted. "Anyway, the one in Stuttgart spoke English."

"Mercenaries, then," Kettering replied. "If they don't want to be connected with the raids, they use a foreigner."

"I've never heard of GSG-9 using outside help."

"Or what about Mossad?"

"Don't you think Mossad could find an agent who speaks fluent German?" Jodl asked.

"They could be working with the CIA," Kettering offered. "Or perhaps they want to cast suspicion on the Americans. A trick like that would have appeal in Tel Aviv."

"I sometimes wonder, Hans, if you're not—"

The gunshot interrupted Jodl, and he bolted from his chair. Kettering rose in a flash to stand beside him, reaching for the pistol on his belt.

"They've found us, Gunter," Kettering cried.

"It could just be someone with an itchy trigger finger."

"My men wouldn't—"

"What? Make a mistake? They haven't done too well so far."

There was more shooting, and Jodl left Kettering stammering a lame defense for his soldiers. He moved toward the window and saw one of the guards run past, followed by another, weapons ready in their hands.

Jodl had a dozen men outside, and six or seven in the house. He hoped that it would be enough.

BOLAN HEARD THE FIRST report of gunfire when he was still eighty yards from Jodl's house. It sounded like a gunshot. It wasn't a weapon Josef Pries was carrying, which meant that he was almost certainly the target.

The only thing to do now was to rush the house with all deliberate speed, keep after Jodl and pray that the German cop could take care of himself.

He wore his nightsuit, his face and hands covered with combat cosmetics, and carried the silenced Uzi, the Walther P-1 automatic, extra magazines, a razor-edged stiletto and grenades. The Executioner meant this probe to be his final raid in Germany, and he was pulling out all the stops to get it right.

Bolan followed the sound of someone running, to his left. He came up on the runner's blind side, almost breathing down his neck, and recognized the skinhead from his shiny scalp, the boots, blue jeans and leather jacket. He resembled something from a 1950s television show, but there was nothing out-of-date about the AK-47 in his hands.

The runner caught sight of Bolan, who shot him from six or seven paces out. The skinhead seemed to pick up speed before his legs turned to rubber and he went down. The folding-stock Kalashnikov bounced on the grass, and Bolan grabbed it on the fly, looping the sling across one shoulder as he kept on running toward the house.

With forty yards to go to the house Bolan surprised another skinhead sentry running to assist his comrades. He had no time to react before a burst of parabellum manglers opened up his chest and dropped him writhing on the grass. Bolan claimed the long, curved magazine from the sentry's rifle and tucked it in his belt.

A blaze of floodlights had brought the house to life, lighting up the grounds as bright as day. Two gunners were stationed at the front door, one a skinhead in his early twenties, carrying a short Beretta submachine gun, and an older, ordinary-looking man who held a shotgun with the stock braced on his hip, its muzzle pointed toward the sky. They'd have a clear view of the ground Bolan would be crossing toward the house, but it would cost him precious time to circle around in the hope of finding an unguarded approach.

He let the Uzi dangle on its shoulder sling and checked the AK-47, making sure it was cocked and locked. The Russian piece would make no end of noise, but by the time it registered and brought the others running, he hoped to be inside the house.

It was a clear break over open ground, and Bolan ran flat-out, the AK-47 leading.

The skinhead spotted Bolan first and barked a warning to his sidekick as he raised his stubby SMG. The older man's response was smooth, professional...but not quite good enough.

The AK-47 came to life in Bolan's hands, bright flame erupting from the muzzle as he charged his adversaries, firing from the hip. The 7.62 mm rounds hit hard from sixty feet, exploding into flesh and bone with crushing force. The skinhead vaulted backward and collided with the older gunman, both of them collapsing as the storm of metal-jacketed projectiles took them down.

The steps were slick with blood when Bolan reached the front door. It was unlocked, and he shouldered through into an entry hall with hanging tapestries on either wall and polished hardwood underfoot. A few steps farther he reached the entrance to a lavish sunken parlor. He was halfway down the steps when someone cut loose with a submachine gun from behind the couch.

HANS KETTERING WAS worried and excited. It pleased him that his men would have a chance to prove themselves, redeem their honor after the disastrous events that went before.

The thought of a decisive victory was thrilling, but he also felt a pang of fear when he considered what would happen if they lost. A fresh defeat, with Gunter Jodl looking on, was bound to mean the end of Jodl's monthly payoff to the cause.

More to the point, Kettering was worried what would happen to himself if this turned out to be another rout. The shame in front of Jodl would be one thing, but he feared more the prospect of a sudden, violent death. In his world, pain and bloodshed were reserved for those inferiors who tried to take advantage of the master race. It was enough that he should lend his wits and energy, his natural charisma and his knack for solving thorny problems. Someone else could do the heavy fighting, while he occupied a place of honor in the stands and cheered them on.

But not this time.

The fight had come to him, and there would be no opportunity for him to slip away. Jodl would regard it as a sign of weakness, and he might begin to think in terms of choosing a new leader for the Front. That wouldn't do, and Kettering made up his mind to face the fear that dogged him.

Leaving Jodl in the library, he went out through the kitchen and across the flagstone patio to find out what was happening. Mossad, GSG-9, or CIA, he didn't really believe their adversaries would commit a major force to the assault upon a well-known German businessman. More soldiers meant more targets and a greater chance of someone being killed or captured. The media would run with this, whichever way it went, and covert agencies were notoriously camera shy.

The sounds of battle were concentrated on the east side of the house, around the corner. Kettering ran in that direction, tugging the SIG-Sauer from its holster, drawing back the hammer with his thumb. If he could only be there at the kill, perhaps provide the coup de grace, he'd stand tall in Jodl's eyes, a soldier taking care of business.

He went around the corner, conscious of a sudden stillness. The guns had all shut down at once, and for an instant Kettering was worried that he might have arrived too late.

A solitary stranger stood before him, wielding a submachine gun. On the ground lay three skinheads and a man from Jodl's private guard, their bodies twisted in the awkward attitudes of sudden death. Blood was everywhere, like fresh paint spattered on their clothes, pale flesh, the grass.

Kettering felt his stomach knotting as the stranger raised his head. Their eyes met, locked and held.

He made it thirty feet between them, half that distance to the corner of the house and sanctuary, but knew he'd never make it if he turned his back and ran. He'd be cut down without a second thought, and everyone who saw his body afterward would know that he died running from the fight. If there was no way out, at least he could attempt to take the bastard with him, maybe catch a stroke of luck and do the job where his men had failed.

He raised the pistol, sighting down the slide, and was about to fire when something struck him hard and deep below the waistline. Pain like white-hot coals seared through him, spoiled his aim and sent the single bullet whining into space. Gravity dragged Kettering to his knees. He felt a warm wetness filling up his pants, then saw a dark stain spreading on the front of them and soaking through the fabric of his shirt. He toppled over on his face and lay there, tasting grass, until a boot wormed underneath one arm and rolled him over on his back.

"Hans Kettering?" the stranger asked him, bending down to meet the dying skinhead's bleary gaze.

Kettering couldn't answer. He tried to nod but had no idea if he succeeded. It didn't matter. Nothing mattered anymore.

Josef Pries stood for a brief moment, then headed toward the house.

THE PARLOR FLOOR WAS HARD on his knees and elbows, smooth from countless polishings, but Bolan found some traction and scuttled for the cover of an oversized easy chair. A second burst of gunfire rattled overhead, perhaps six inches from the mark, and he was thankful for the gunner's haste. With a bit more care, the man would have had him cold.

He gauged the direction from the sound of firing and a brief glimpse of his enemy before he hit the floor. A sniping duel could take forever, coming down to luck or numbers, or the supply of ammunition each man carried. Bolan had another plan in mind.

He reached down for a frag grenade, unclipped it from his belt and threw the safety pin away. Clenched fingers held the spoon in place. Bolan got his bearings, calculating the velocity and angle he would need to make it work.

He made the pitch a classic up-and-over, lofting the grenade for altitude instead of distance. One glimpse of his hand, and Bolan's enemy squeezed off another burst that drilled the armchair, sending cotton stuffing into the air before he ducked out of sight. The guy was cautious, cheating Bolan of a target, but he hadn't counted on the lethal egg that fell beside him, bounced once on the floor and started wobbling like an awkward toy.

The blast rocked Bolan, laced the easy chair with shrapnel and left cordite hanging heavy in the air. He came up with the AK-47, ready to see the lacerated body of the gunner sprawled like a rag doll, several yards from where he'd been crouching when the bomb went off.

It was a short sprint to the stairs, but Bolan didn't have to go that far. Instead, he glimpsed a man retreating toward the kitchen. He recognized his profile from a photo in the Bundespolizei files. Gunter Jodl was a little heavier, a little older than he'd been in the photograph, but there was no mistake.

A dozen strides and he reached the kitchen door, still swinging on its hinges. Bolan went in firing and saw his target dive behind a stand-up freezer. Jodl returned fire with an automatic. Bolan ducked underneath the first two rounds and found cover in the shadow of a heavy butcher's block.

The Executioner was prepared to use another frag grenade, when Jodl gave him something else to think about. The pimp's third shot glanced off a copper pot and sent it flying, causing several cans to topple from atop the butcher's block. One bounced off Bolan's shoulder, and another nearly brained him before it hit the floor.

He palmed the can and hefted it, gears meshing in his head. A slow smile spread across his face as he peeled the paper label from the can.

It was another easy pitch—anywhere within a yard or so of Jodl would be close enough. As Bolan made the toss, he yelled, *"Grenaden!"*

Jodl burst from cover with a cry of panic, squeezing off a wild shot as he ran. The AK-47 caught him halfway to the exit, heavy bullets ripping into him and spinning him.

It was over in a heartbeat, all except the walk-through to make sure that Bolan was leaving no one in position for a clear shot at his back. Outside, he found Pries waiting for him near the porch, his submachine gun covering the door.

"All done?" Pries asked him.

"Looks that way."

Pries cocked a thumb in the direction of approaching sirens. "I think it's time for us to go."

11

Day was breaking as they stood beside their separate cars in Aachen, thirty miles west of Cologne, near the point where Germany, Belgium and Holland came together. It was light enough for Bolan to make out an angry purple bruise on Pries's forehead, near the hairline.

"Someone tagged you," he remarked.

"My fault," Pries said. "I got too close, and one of them was faster than I counted on. He swung around and nearly took my head off with his shotgun barrel. Next time, I'll shoot first."

"Next time?"

Pries shook his head. "I didn't mean...."

"I know exactly what you meant."

The silence stretched between them like a cobweb, growing thinner and more tenuous.

"I think it'll be very quiet here without you," Pries finally said.

"Don't bet your pension on it," Bolan answered. "Quiet's relative. You've still got lots of work to do."

It wasn't criticism, nor did Pries take it that way. "Does it ever end?" he asked.

"It hasn't yet for me. You might have better luck."

"I don't think I believe in luck," Pries told him. "Once I did, but these days the only luck I see is bad."

"We make our own," Bolan said.

"Do you believe that?"

Bolan nodded. "Preparation, planning and a dash of circumstance. It works for me."

Pries leaned against his car and stared toward the border. "I'll have to think about what I should say in my report. The truth will never do."

"You might want to debrief before you tackle anything on paper. Chances are, the brass would just as soon forget the whole thing happened."

"Wash their hands like Pilate, hmm? It wouldn't be the first time."

"If they try to set you up, there's not much I can do to help," Bolan said.

"It won't be necessary," Pries answered. "I haven't survived the politics this long without learning—how do you say?—where the bodies are buried?"

"That's what we say."

"When will you rest, my friend?"

"I'm getting there," the Executioner replied. "A few more days."

"You should be going, I imagine."

"Right."

There was no more to say. They shook hands, then got into their cars. Bolan had a parting glimpse of Pries in his rearview mirror, one hand raised, before the highway whisked him out of sight.

The border crossing wasn't difficult. He showed the customs men a passport in the name of Mike Belasko, told them he was traveling on pleasure and would be in Holland for only a day or two. He had no fixed address in mind and meant to go as the spirit moved him. When the customs agent handed back his passport with a smile, it seemed sincere.

Indeed, from his experience on prior excursions, Bolan knew the Dutch to be efficient, tidy, organized and courteous. Their country had long been a crossroads for travel and trade. An endless series of invasions—by the Romans, Saxons, Franks, Napoleon, the Nazi Wehrmacht and sundry tourists—had imbued the Dutch with patience and a great facility for languages. A traveler from almost any point in North America or Western Europe could relax in Holland, confident that he'd have no difficulty in communicating with his gracious hosts.

Unfortunately Bolan's visit this time wasn't a pleasure trip. And those he sought were something less than courteous behind the masks they wore in public. They were dealers in pornography and prostitution, both legal, but they weren't satisfied with native volunteers. Instead, they cast their nets abroad, paid well for women—even children—who weren't inclined to ask for help from the police.

It was an old system, tested over centuries, from China to the Middle East and all points in between. The human cattle were purchased from their families with bogus offers of employment, or forcibly abducted, if the risk of prosecution could be minimized. Once under lock and key, the chosen were "broken in" by nonstop sexual assault, most commonly with some narcotic introduced to ease the pain and cultivate dependence. By the time a working girl was "seasoned," the combined effects of drug addiction, shame, intimidation and pervasive hopelessness reduced her to a walking zombie, going through the motions on command. Few customers complained, and the police didn't concern themselves with "voluntary'' prostitutes, as long as they paid taxes and secured the proper work permits.

One Danish group, called Freedom's Flower, had done everything within its power to subvert the flesh trade—filing multiple petitions with the UN and the World Court at The Hague; reporting proved and suspected crimes to Dutch police; enlisting spokesmen for Amnesty International and the World Antislavery Society to publicize the plight of foreign prostitutes in Amsterdam, Rotterdam and elsewhere. The group's activities were noted in the major daily newspapers, but the trade suffered no great inconvenience from a few arrests of smugglers, low-grade pimps and drugged-out hookers who refused to testify against their masters.

Bosnia had changed that, to some extent, with spotlights focused on the rape camps and ethnic cleansing. When Muslim women from Bosnia had started turning up in Holland, Freedom's Flower cast around for someone to help them shut the pipeline down, and Brognola and the team at Stony Man Farm had gotten involved.

Freedom's Flower had arranged for a contact to be waiting for him in Utrecht. Her name was Anika Doorn, and Bolan knew a little of her background: wealthy parents, both deceased now, with a handsome trust fund to support her while she found her way in life; no siblings; back-to-back degrees in sociology and law from one of Holland's finest universities. Doorn had drafted most of the petitions filed by Freedom's Flower in the past four years, but apparently she became frustrated as her faith in working through the system had begun to fail.

Now she was waiting for an executioner to help in ways the system never could.

And Bolan found that he was looking forward to the last round of the game.

"I DON'T LIKE MYSTERIES," Willem Ruud said through the fat cigar clenched in his teeth. "You know that, don't you, Jani?"

"Yes, Willem." Jani van Zon knew it very well indeed.

"At first we thought it was the Germans, playing games in Bosnia so they could dominate the traffic. Now, I turn on the television and they themselves are dead. What are your thoughts on this matter?"

"I don't know."

"You don't know. I must confess to ignorance myself, of course. There's no shame in that, providing we make every effort to resolve the problem. Quickly. Do we understand each other, Jani?"

"Sir?"

"We can't take chances. Approximately how much did we make last year?"

"Fifty million guilders."

"Fifty million. After taxes, bribes and overhead, that's—what? Say fifteen million, free and clear."

"Eighteen."

"Eighteen. Do you enjoy your life-style, Jani?"

"Yes, Willem."

"As do I. You prefer your little flat on Marnixstraat to being locked up in a cell, I take it?"

"Certainly."

"And any house at all is preferable to being dead, am I correct?"

"Yes, sir."

"From what we've seen in Bosnia and Germany, someone—let us say the enemy—is more concerned with killing off our friends than sending them to prison. You agree with that?" Ruud asked.

"It seems to be the case."

"So, we must ask ourselves if he—or they—will be satisfied with Serbs and Germans. Will the killing stop? Or is there someone on the way to see us?"

"I don't know, Willem."

"There you are. A failure of intelligence. We haven't been efficient in this matter, Jani. I take my share of responsibility, despite the fact that you are paid—and very handsomely, I'd say—to deal with problems of this nature. I have been too lax in supervising you. I will not make the same mistake again."

"No."

"See if you can find any of the survivors in Cologne. Have someone speak to the police. I want to know *exactly* what became of our associates—how they were killed, what steps they took in self-defense, what measures they forgot to take. If there was any pattern to the attacks, we need to know about it. I want details. Nothing whatsoever must be left to chance. Do you understand?"

"Yes, Willem."

"Then get on with it."

Ruud found that he preferred to be alone these days, when there were problems weighing on his mind. If he had questions, he could summon people with the answers. Otherwise, he disliked having hangers-on around him, offering advice when none was sought or wanted, spewing flattery so obvious it turned his stomach. If he made an error, it would be his own, with no one else to blame. And if he won a victory, the glory would be his, as well.

He was concerned, of course; that much was only natural. The raids in Bosnia and Germany were bad for business, but they hadn't cost him much, so far. The inconvenience of arranging new connections and negotiating prices he'd taken in his stride. It was a fact of life for any businessman. Most didn't face the prospect of assassination, though, and he'd have to take that problem seriously if he meant to stay alive.

These were skillful men, no doubt about it, to have come this far and killed so many without losing any of their own. That didn't mean their lives were charmed, however. They'd suffer, and die like any other man—but first, they had to be identified and singled out.

Ruud trusted van Zon to perform the task he'd assigned, but it wasn't enough to scour Bosnia and Germany for clues, something that might take days or even weeks to complete. Meanwhile, the clock could be running out on his life. He had enemies here in Holland. Most had thus far pledged themselves to legal action, with a few misguided demonstrations in the red-light quarters, but who knew when plans might change? Frustration, anger, jealousy and greed were mighty motivators. Any one of them could drive someone to the brink of violence. A combination of those factors was enough to start a war.

So far, Ruud's battery of lawyers had conducted his defense. The law was on his side, unless the opposition could prove that his licensed prostitutes and porno movie stars were being held and forced to work against their will. No single case had made that point to date, although a few weak links had been removed along the way to reinforce the chain. An overdose of drugs, a suicide, perhaps an accidental fall or hit-and-run. Survivors got the point and held their tongues.

As for police, they were content to see the system operating smoothly, quietly, without a lot of bother. No one but the vultures of the press adored a scandal, and for Ruud's part, he'd just as soon leave the headlines to the British, Americans and French. In Holland liberty had found its place with order, and the two ideals were perfectly compatible—as long as strong men kept the peace.

One step in that direction would be to weed out the malcontents who raised a hue and cry where none was justified. Ruud had a notion where to start, and he wasn't averse to striking first, before his enemies drew blood in Holland. With a bit of luck, one swift, decisive stroke might save a world of trouble later on.

It would be best not to trouble van Zon, who had such pressing matters on his mind already. There were specialists to do this kind of thing, and Ruud knew them all.

He reached for the phone, tapped a number out and waited as the distant ringing began.

ANIKA DOORN WAS NERVOUS now that the time was fast approaching for her meeting with the stranger who had come so far, and dared so much, to help her cause. No, that wasn't correct. Not *her* cause, but the cause of freedom.

She was aware, to some extent, of what was happening in Germany. Familiar names had leaped out at her from the early news reports that morning: Gunter Jodl and his Nazi toad, Hans Kettering were both dead, along with others from their syndicate.

Doorn had been desperate when she'd asked for help from the United States. She'd tried other angles but in vain. The Dutch police could find no grounds for prosecution. Interpol was interested only in hard evidence of a specific crime. At the United Nations, they had permanent committees to assess reports of slavery and human-rights violations, but they were more concerned with child labor than sexual exploitation—and, in the final analysis, they had no power to enforce decrees against offending parties. The World Court, so close at hand, was likewise powerless. It had no authority beyond its chambers, no enforcement arm to make a verdict stick.

It seemed to be a hopeless case until a sympathetic officer with Interpol suggested she might try speaking to a man in the United States. This man had been helpful with problem cases that exceeded Interpol's legitimate authority. The suspects in those cases rarely came to trial alive, but even so...

For Doorn anything was better than another fat-cat politician smiling at her, telling her that there was nothing anyone could do within the law. She'd join forces with the devil, if another woman, or one more child, could be saved from the flesh trade's vortex.

It took thirteen days between her conversation with the man from Interpol and the return call to her home. It had been a woman's voice, she'd thought, perhaps distorted electronically, dictating dates, times and places. Later, when she'd tried to check, Doorn had found the call had come from Amsterdam, but that was easily arranged, she knew, with relays, cutouts and the like.

Still, the message had been clear enough. Unless another call directed otherwise, she should expect a visitor on one of three specific days. She was to meet him at the central railway station, wearing a red dress and carrying a fresh bouquet of flowers wrapped in tissue paper. She should let herself be seen around the platform for arrivals from the south. If she wasn't approached between 2:45 and 3:00 p.m., Doorn should return the next day, and the next.

It was the third day now, and she'd wasted two bouquets already. One more day, and if there was no phone call to explain, Doorn would assume the strangers had abandoned her for reasons of their own.

She slipped on the red dress and pensively stood before the full-length bedroom mirror. The killing troubled her, but she'd reached a point of desperation where the most bizarre solutions merited consideration. If that meant she would be responsible for bloodshed, then Doorn reckoned she'd learn to live with it. Her own part in the drama would be marginal, though, perhaps directing the professionals to certain targets, swallowing her guilt when bodies turned up in the streets and on the television news.

Attempting to distract herself, she wondered what the man would look like. Would he be the classic secret agent or assassin from the movies, the hero who always triumphed in the end? There was no script to follow in real life, however, and she knew from personal experience that wealthy villains had a way of wriggling through the net. If bribery didn't work, they could rely on threats, coercion, even murder to achieve their goals. The heroes, meanwhile, were restricted in their choice of methods by established law.

Unless, perhaps, you found a covert agency that lived to bend the rules, sometimes ignored them altogether in pursuit of a selected target. Groups like that were no simple thing to track down, and Doorn thanked heaven for her luck and made a silent vow that she'd keep her personal misgivings and any guilty feelings to herself. If it worked out, her sacrifice of conscience would be worth it. If it failed...well, she'd be no worse off than when she'd started.

The railway station in downtown Utrecht was crowded when Bolan pulled into the parking lot at 2:15 p.m. He'd taken his time on the sixty-mile drive from the border, stopping for food and to top off the gas tank, watching his mirror for tails and generally killing time like a tourist with nowhere to go in a hurry. He'd left himself some extra minutes before his rendezvous to look around and make sure there was no ambush waiting in the wings.

He didn't spot any suspicious persons in the parking lot, no gunners standing by to close the trap behind him when he passed. The men who killed for money ran to type, at least in attitude, the chill and grim determination in their eyes. Cool weather meant that nearly everyone he passed wore coats or sweaters, but he kept an eye out for the telltale bulges that would signal hidden weapons.

By the time he reached the terminal, he'd relaxed a bit. But he wouldn't feel entirely safe until he met Anika Doorn, got her away from there and verified that no one followed from the terminal.

He dawdled through the depot proper, checking out the ticket lines, the newsstand, the tourists clustered at the snack bar. Nothing was out of place that he could see. A lone policeman circulated through the crowd, and Bolan wondered whether he had backup on the premises, or if he would be forced to telephone for help should anything go wrong.

He drifted toward the platform where the train from Amsterdam would be arriving at 2:35 p.m. Dutch trains were never late, except in cases of derailment or mechanical malfunction, and exacting maintenance routines made such occasions few and far between. It all depended on his contact now, and whether she would keep their rendezvous.

He spotted Doorn at 2:29, the red of her dress standing out clearly. From the first glimpse of her face and figure, blond hair falling free around her shoulders, Bolan knew the dress and the bunch of flowers in her hand had been redundant. She would hardly pass unnoticed in a crowd.

Doorn was approaching Bolan's end of the platform. She didn't appear to be nervous. She kept the flowers—tulips, Bolan noted—in one hand; the other held the thin strap of a purse she wore slung across her shoulder.

He waited, letting her travel half the length of the arrivals platform. She ignored the terminal, barely casting a glance at the crowd and stood waiting for the train from Amsterdam. He wondered if the woman knew her part that well, or if she really thought that he was coming by rail.

He would join her in a moment, at the appointed time, speak the coded phrase and wait to hear the correct response. From there it was a short walk to the parking lot and Bolan's car. If she resisted, he'd tell her that the depot wasn't safe for their discussion, with so many eyes and ears around. She'd understand...or he'd walk away and leave her with no choice but to pursue him if she meant to carry on with the deal.

Bolan's jacket was unbuttoned, granting rapid access to the Walther P-1 automatic in its armpit holster if the need arose. It always lingered at the back of his mind that a simple meeting could go wrong, degenerate into a massacre in seconds flat. Still, he was hoping for an easy touch.

Until he saw the shooters on Doorn's tail.

FOR ALL HER SEEMING confidence, Doorn was beginning to feel self-conscious in the low-cut, sleeveless red dress. It was cool, and she'd left her sweater in the car in case the man she was supposed to meet wouldn't be able to recognize her with it on.

She checked her watch: 2:33 p.m. From the general stirring in the crowd, she knew the train was on its way. Doorn drifted with the crowd. There was no harm in acting natural while she waited for her contact.

She jumped when strong, rough fingers closed about her arm, exerting painful pressure. When she spun, the stranger was smiling at her, revealing crooked rows of teeth.

WIT DEKKER DIDN'T MIND the rush job. He was used to being called when someone discovered an emergency that couldn't wait. In fact his livelihood depended on emergencies like that.

And he never failed to satisfy. He knew he was worth the fees he charged, beginning at a base of fifty thousand guilders and proceeding up the scale from there, depending on the project's difficulty, special orders from his client and the target's status in society.

It was no big deal to kill a woman in her thirties, given time to plan and room to operate, but Willem Ruud had called for swift results—before the sun went down. That raised the price, as it increased Dekker's risk and forced him to employ two helpers for the job. On top of that he knew the target was a somewhat controversial figure, known for agitation in the legislature and public demonstration in the red-light districts. She had to be eliminated in a way that wouldn't instantly reflect on Ruud—or Dekker, for that matter.

With Koenraad driving and Deman in the back seat with the gear, they'd pulled up in front of Anika Doorn's apartment building. She was just emerging onto the street, and Dekker judged that it would cause too much disturbance if they tried to grab her on the spot. Much better, they'd decided, to follow her awhile and see where she was going. Something would suggest itself; maybe she'd stop somewhere to use the telephone, with no witnesses nearby. Whatever happened, they'd have to make the pickup smooth and silent, with no commotion that would prompt a call to the police. Anika Doorn was meant to disappear without a trace.

They trailed her to the railway station. Dekker thought of grabbing her before she left the parking lot, but Koenraad got them stuck behind a minivan, and he didn't care to make the move in front of witnesses. Instead, they parked the car and walked toward the terminal—like any other businessmen who had to catch a train.

Their target obviously didn't plan to take the train herself. She had no luggage with her, and the small bouquet she carried spoke of greeting rather than departure. It was one more complication, running up the odds, but Dekker had his orders. She had to die this day, and no mistake. If they were forced to take a friend along, so be it. Two could disappear almost as easily as one.

The hard part, Dekker knew, would be the snatch itself. One person lifted from a busy railroad terminal was tricky; lifting two without a fuss verged on impossible. Still, it was better than letting them drive away and risk being forced to stop Doorn's car in traffic, with a crowd of angry drivers leaning on their horns and memorizing license numbers.

Dekker took the north end of the platform, Deman trailing Koenraad to the south. With five minutes left before the train from Amsterdam arrived, they started closing on the woman.

Dekker slipped the button on his jacket, feeling the H&K P-7 automatic warm against his belly. None of them were packing silencers, and he'd have to keep his fingers crossed that Doorn offered no resistance. If she struggled, he'd have to knock her out as economically as possible. A solid blow behind the ear, perhaps, or a modified choke hold disguised as a lover's embrace.

He came up on her blind side, caught her right arm in his left, the little automatic covered in his right. Doorn turned to him, Dekker smiled.

"You'll come with us," he said, letting her feel the pistol jammed against her ribs.

Just before all hell broke loose.

THERE HAD TO BE WORSE places for a firefight, but the crowded railway platform offered special problems of its own. Aside from the civilians already on hand, more would soon be spilling from the train when it arrived. The engineer would have no way of telling that the depot had become a war zone. Dozens of people could be killed or wounded if the play got out of hand.

By the same token Bolan couldn't afford to wait and let the heavies take Anika. He couldn't tell what their intentions were, but they were armed, and one of them had already drawn his weapon as he stood beside the woman, reaching out to grasp her arm. Another moment, and he might just be too late.

It was a judgment call, and Bolan made his move. He came in from behind the nearest gunner, slamming a solid elbow shot into the point where skull and collar met. The guy went down, not quite unconscious, but he lost his grip on both the woman and the automatic simultaneously. Bolan grabbed Anika's arm and spun her toward the station terminal.

"This way!" he snapped, allowing her no room for argument.

A swift backward glance showed that the other two gunners were drawing for their weapons, one moving toward his fallen comrade, while the second made to follow Bolan and Doorn. The show of hardware started people shouting, jostling one another as they tried to get out of the way.

Still, the first shot sounded unnaturally loud. The bullet hummed past Bolan and struck a portly man just stepping from the terminal. He fell backward, taking down two other people as he fell. The cries of alarm unraveled into screams as Bolan turned and drew his pistol, lining up his shot, the fingers of his free hand locked around his companion's wrist.

The gunman saw it coming and tried to move away, but he couldn't escape the press of humanity. A head shot would have been the way to go, but Bolan couldn't risk a miss. He slammed a shot into the gunner's stomach, saw him double over and drop in a fetal curl.

That still left two, but killing them was less important than escaping from the terminal. Every second counted, and Bolan could hear the numbers running as he dragged Doorn after him across the main room of the terminal.

Away to Bolan's left, the uniformed patrolman he'd noticed earlier was running toward them, a revolver in his hand, and shouting what could only be commands for them to halt. Avoiding him would be more difficult than ducking the assassins, since the use of lethal force wasn't an option. Bolan wouldn't fire on a policeman, period, no matter what the provocation, but he wouldn't waste time on negotiation, either.

In the end one of his adversaries solved the problem for him. Bolan had Doorn veering toward the nearest doorway, trying to outrun the cop, when gunshots echoed through the terminal. He turned in time to see the officer go down, a sprawling rag-doll figure, lost in the stampede of would-be passengers as they ran screaming for the exits.

Bolan crouched, pulling his companion down beside him, and waited for the crowd to part and let him see his target. Any shot at all would do. He didn't even have to kill the man, just slow him enough to let them reach the parking lot intact.

And there he was, a chunky figure weaving through the crush of bodies, striking out to right and left as he came after Bolan and Doorn. The gunner's face was beet-red and slick with sweat.

The Walther P-1 bucked in Bolan's hand: once, twice. He saw the bullets strike their target in the upper chest and shoulder, spinning him until he hit the floor.

"Come on!"

They made another mad dash for the exit, getting shoved and jostled all the way. Outside, Bolan made a beeline for the parking lot, Doorn close behind him. He could hear her gasping, trying to keep up. There was at least one shooter still alive somewhere behind them, and the Executioner wasn't about to gamble on his being down and out.

They reached the car, and Bolan had his keys in hand. He opened the driver's door, then stood back to let Doorn slide across the seat. She hesitated, staring at him, worry in her eyes.

"Do you believe in fighting windmills?" Bolan asked.

Relief showed on her face as she responded to the password. "It depends upon the cause."

"We haven't got a lot of time to hang around," he told her.

"But, my car—"

"It should be safe for now. A few more minutes and half the cops in Utrecht will be on the scene."

"You're right."

She climbed into the car, and Bolan slid behind the wheel. A moment later they were rolling. Only when the terminal was well behind them, and the rearview mirror gave no indication of a tail, did Bolan let himself relax.

It was a poor beginning, but the woman was alive and well. He'd pick things up from there.

"I don't suppose you recognized those men," Bolan said after they'd driven several miles in silence.

"No," Doorn answered, "but I know who sent them."

"That's as good a place to start as any."

"Willem Ruud," she said. "You know the name?"

"I got a briefing," Bolan told her, calling up a mental image of the photographs he'd been shown at Stony Man. "I'll need whatever details you can give me."

"He lives in Amsterdam, but he has contacts throughout the country—throughout Europe and beyond. He's never been arrested, and you can call that equal parts of luck and influence. My understanding is that Ruud made his first million guilders in narcotics, then decided that the business was too risky after several of his cohorts went to prison. Prostitution and pornography are legal in our country, as you know. Ruud found a way to lower costs and beat the competition on variety."

"With slaves," Bolan said. It wasn't a question.

"Right. He started shopping in the Philippines, Thailand, wherever daughters are a liability to parents facing economic hardship. He smuggles women in by several routes and has official documents on hand for them when they arrive—work visas, birth certificates, whatever they require. The documents aren't forgeries, per se. He buys them from the government en masse and fills them out himself, then bribes someone in immigration for a stamp to make things legal."

"He's been branching out from Asian stock," Bolan remarked.

"Yes. Some of his customers—most of them, I suppose—prefer to sleep with European women as a rule. They sample Africans and Asians for variety, but mostly they keep sexual relations on their own side of the color bar. The civil war in Bosnia was heaven-sent for Ruud. If there was no such thing as ethnic cleansing, I've no doubt he would invent it."

"What a prince."

"He's scum," she said with unexpected vehemence. "We know what he's doing from our conversations with competitors and a few of Ruud's own women. Getting them to testify in court is hopeless, though, as you can well imagine."

"Bad for business," Bolan said dryly.

"And for their health. As for the other pimps, while they would love to see Ruud locked away, they have a code of silence where police and prosecutors are concerned. Aside from practical considerations, they're also frightened of the power Ruud can wield."

Bolan thought about that for another block or so before he said, "I'm not concerned with legal testimony."

"So I gathered."

Something in the woman's tone stopped just this side of flat-out disapproval. She seemed to be having qualms, but Bolan thought she had a fair grip on herself, considering his mission and the circumstances of their meeting.

"I assume you're clear on what it is I do," he said.

She frowned and nodded. "I've been following the news from Germany."

"Were you surprised?"

"Not really. Disappointed that it's come to this, perhaps. I made the call, and I accept the consequences."

"That sounds good in theory," Bolan said, "but can you live with it?"

"You make it sound as if I have a choice."

"We all have choices," he reminded her.

"Such as?"

"You say the word, and I'll stop the car right here. Or I can drive you to the airport and put you on a flight to the country of your choice. You can relax awhile, come back next week and never mind what happens while you're gone."

"Is it that easy?" Doorn asked. "Shutting out responsibility, I mean?"

"It never worked for me," Bolan admitted.

"You need my help, I think. With directions and information."

"Only if you've got it in you," Bolan replied.

"I don't have a choice. Please understand, the others in our movement don't know anything about this. Most of them would be horrified. But they've been after Ruud for close to three years, now, two years for me. The police type out reports and put them in a file somewhere. For all I know they never even speak to Ruud—except to thank him for his large donations to their various insurance funds and charities. Three years, and not a single charge has been laid against him. I can name at least five women who have died within that time because of Willem Ruud. Officially their deaths are down as suicide or accidental causes, but their blood is on his hands.''

''Okay,'' the Executioner said. ''Let's start spreading it around.''

''YOU SHOULD HAVE LET ME do it, Willem.''

Jani van Zon's tone was terse, but civil. It was no good shouting at the boss. In fact it could be downright lethal.

''You were busy,'' Ruud informed him. ''I admire your talents, Jani, but you can't be everywhere at once.''

''I would have done it right the first time.''

''Spare me the recriminations, will you? Dekker's been of use to use before. I needn't tell you that.''

''For simple killings. This was different.''

''So I gather.''

Two men dead, Dekker nearly bagged by the police and they'd missed their target. Now Anika Doorn was hiding somewhere, on her guard, and from the fragmentary information Dekker had passed along, it was a safe bet that she had at least one ally. A fighter this time, not the pacifists and pamphleteers she worked with on a daily basis. This was much more dangerous, Ruud thought.

''I understand the risk involved,'' Ruud went on.

''Have the police connected Dekker to the dead men?'' van Zon asked.

''He's not a total imbecile.'' Ruud didn't sound convinced though. ''There will be witnesses, of course. It can't be helped. But with all the confusion, I wouldn't count on anything of substance.''

"Dekker isn't the concern," van Zon replied. "You thought it was important to remove the woman. It is all the more important now, seeing we've missed her once."

The "we" was a deliberate ploy, van Zon accepting his share of responsibility for the disaster Ruud and Dekker had concocted on their own. In van Zon's mind, it gave him an advantage, made him feel superior to Ruud in some way he couldn't really define. Dumb luck had spared him from participating in the bungled kidnapping that would, he hoped, result in Dekker being barred from working with the syndicate.

"Between the two of us," Ruud said, "I'm more concerned than ever. She has friends now—one, at least—and not the sort we're used to. Dekker's men weren't the smartest, but they knew their business. They weren't eliminated by a lucky novice."

"I can find her," van Zon stated with more assurance than he felt. It was important to present a bold front now, when Willem needed him the most. "We know her friends, the others in her movement. One of them will surely know where she's gone."

"I hope so," Ruud replied. "We can't expect to buy these friends of hers, and I don't think they'll simply go away."

"The men from Germany?" van Zon asked.

"Maybe not the same, but close enough. We've seen what they can do."

The more he thought about it, the more van Zon was convinced their enemy in Holland had to be the same men who'd executed their associates in Bosnia and Germany. It seemed only logical. Otherwise, coincidence was strained a mile beyond the breaking point, and common sense flew out the window.

"I'm not afraid," he boasted. "I'll find these men and kill them for you, Willem."

"I sincerely hope so, Jani. As for Dekker..."

"He should serve as an example," van Zon said. "Unless we punish him, he'll be laughing at us along with his friends."

That "we" again, but Ruud didn't seem to mind. "I think his closest friends are dead. Maybe he should join them. But nothing obvious," Ruud went on thoughtfully. "We don't want anybody asking questions."

"No." Van Zon was smiling now. "I wouldn't be surprised if Dekker was despondent over losing his associates. Depression makes a man do crazy things."

"Indeed it does. I'll trust your judgment, Jani."

To a point, he almost added, but the words remained unspoken.

"I won't let you down," van Zon replied. "I'll also squeeze the woman's friends until somebody gives her up."

"As you see fit—but cautiously. We don't need any more publicity. God help us if the press gets hold of this."

"There won't be any headlines," van Zon promised. "You have my word."

"Get going, then," Ruud said. "We're wasting time."

The statement that Ruud trusted Jani's judgment was the next best thing to designation of van Zon as heir apparent to the empire. That could change, though, if he didn't carry out his promise in a timely manner.

Where to start?

He knew the men and women who made up the leadership of Freedom's Flower. Early on, before the group began to flourish, van Zon had prepared a hit list of its principals and asked Ruud for permission to eliminate the threat while it was still a flea bite, rather than a gaping sore. Ruud had opted for a course of moderation, counting on his friends and human nature to defeat the Puritan reformers. His strategy had failed; now it was time for van Zon to step in, with more aggressive measures, to redeem the situation.

There was no doubt in his mind that he could do the job. The only question was the number of assorted lowlifes he'd have to kill in the process.

AGAINST HIS BETTER judgment, Bolan drove Doorn back to the railway station's parking lot to pick up her car. The police were everywhere, and she got out a block before they reached the depot, mingling with the crowd and walking in to fetch her car. Nobody tried to stop her as she drove away, and while she worried that they might have copied down her license number, it would be of no help. She wouldn't be at home if anyone came knocking on her door, having discussed with Bolan the hotel she'd be staying in for the time being, which was near the Music Centre.

She had only a little money with her, so she found an automatic teller machine and withdrew two thousand guilders from her bank account to tide her over. Dutch hotels demanded passports from their foreign guests, but the locals could use any name they liked, as long as they were paying cash. Doorn got a reasonable rate at the hotel and pretended that her bags were in the car. In fact there was a shopping mall not far away, and she could pick up some essentials—food included—after nightfall.

In the meantime there was nothing left to do but wait...and think.

She understood that Death had come within a hair of claiming her that afternoon. Without the help of Mike Belasko, she'd certainly be dead—or worse, a prisoner of Willem Ruud—by now. It was a chilling thought, but she was more unnerved when she considered her alliance with the tall American. Belasko was straightforward when he spoke of his intentions. Nothing in the way of details, but he got the point across.

No prisoners. No quarter asked or offered.

This was war.

It was incredible, Doorn thought, that she could put such ominous events in motion with a phone call. Up to now, she'd begun to doubt her own abilities, the failure of her efforts to dispose of Willem Ruud by legal means.

Until this day.

Somehow the foiled attempt on her life had given her new focus, new determination. If the slavers were that desperate, they had to be hurting. It was their turn to be worried for a change.

Of course, she realized that any desperation Ruud might feel was due to Belasko's efforts, not her own. Still, it was Doorn who had set things in motion. If she didn't wield a gun herself, at least she could take partial credit for the end result.

And she'd also share the blame for the events that would inevitably rock her native land within the next few hours. She didn't have nightmares yet about the violence, but Doorn feared that they were coming.

Regardless, she had wasted time enough while Willem Ruud and those who served him fattened their bank accounts from human suffering. The moral question could be left to others.

The brooding urge to violence that Doorn felt inside herself was a surprise. Since the attempt upon her life, she'd focused on the notion of revenge against her enemies. She had no chance to face them on her own, of course, but Mike Belasko was her stand-in. Cool and capable, a hard man even when he smiled, she had no doubt that he could do the job. He was outnumbered, granted, but it would have been the same in Germany—and even worse in Bosnia, where open warfare was the order of the day. If he could live through that and still show up in time to save her life in Utrecht, he had to be a warrior with a will of iron.

He would need that, and more, to survive the next twenty-four hours.

She needed desperately to speak with someone, forge a human contact even as she hid herself from prying eyes. It should be safe to call her best friend in the movement, Mina Carstens. In the past two years they'd developed a relationship that thrived on honesty and steered away from secrets.

Even so, Doorn knew that she wouldn't tell Mina everything. Some secrets weren't meant to be shared.

THE LOCAL NEWS WAS in Dutch, but Bolan picked up bits and pieces, knew the lead would cover his encounter at the railway station. That was fine; his enemies would know about the firefight by this time, and he wasn't concerned about descriptions of himself, as long as no one had the license number of his car. Between the stress of dodging bullets and the built-in contradictions voiced by any group of witnesses to a surprise attack, he had no fear of the police producing sketches that would depict Bolan.

And if they did, well, he'd cope with that eventuality when it arrived. Meanwhile, he had a list of targets ripe for hellfire visitation from the Executioner, and he didn't intend to keep them waiting long.

Anika's list of targets spanned the countryside, from Utrecht, to The Hague, Rotterdam and through to Amsterdam. The list included brothels, out-call offices, hotels where beds were rented by the hour, business fronts controlled by Willem Ruud, the homes of Ruud himself and several ranking members of his syndicate.

In all it would take several days to run the list, but Bolan didn't plan on hitting each and every target. Some of them were small and relatively unimportant to the vice lord's daily take, while others represented sizeable investments. Bolan could have gone directly to Ruud and challenged him at his home, but it suited the Executioner's purpose better to expose the slaver's rotten empire first, and let his neighbors catch a whiff of the corruption in their own backyards before he brought the curtain down.

Bolan thought he might as well begin in Utrecht, just to let his adversaries know Anika Doorn's rescue was no fluke. From there he'd select a few choice targets from the list and spread himself around, creating the illusion of an empire under siege by numerous assailants. By the time Bolan made his way to Amsterdam, Ruud would be feeling heat from his lieutenants in the provinces, perhaps enough to shake him up and breed mistakes.

It took only one slip to kill a man, and Bolan was a master when it came to seizing opportunities in crises.

Let the slaver sweat a little, move his troops around the chessboard if it pleased him, trying to identify his enemy and strike back with sufficient force to end the game. The odds were in the Dutchman's favor, but he had a disadvantage common to a list of others who had come—and gone—before him.

He didn't know that he was dealing with the Executioner.

Assuming Ruud had followed the events in Bosnia and Germany, he was bound to draw a link between the death of his associates and the attacks upon himself. As a creature of the underworld, his first instinct would be to blame competitors, perhaps suspect some rogue police detachment, even vengeful Muslims bent on paying back the man who bought their women. Any one of those assumptions would misdirect Ruud's efforts to defend himself. He'd be wasting vital time and energy in the pursuit of shadows, while an enemy closed the gap between them, moving toward the kill.

It was an edge that Bolan cherished, one that had served him well in similar campaigns around the world. Confusion was as much a weapon as a sniper's bullet or a well-placed frag grenade.

Fatigue checked in with Bolan as he motored toward the first of several targets on his list, reminding him that he was only flesh and blood in spite of the determination that propelled him forward. At some point he'd have to stop and rest, recharge his batteries.

But not just yet.

The Executioner had enemies to kill.

14

The stylish bank at Nieue Gracht 93, in Utrecht, stood within an easy walk of St. Catherine's Convent museum, world famous for its collection of paintings and artifacts tracing the history of Dutch Christianity from the eighth century to modern times.

For Bolan the time had come to put some real heat on his enemies, by striking hard at what they treasured most: their cash reserve.

The time was fifteen minutes shy of closing when he strolled into the bank and took a look around. The standard cameras watched him from three corners of the room, but there were no armed guards in evidence. Armed robbery of banks was such a rarity in Holland that a show of force was deemed unnecessary and, in fact, insulting to the regular customers.

Bolan moved past the tellers' windows, heading toward a glassed-in office on his right. The manager was fifty-something, with a few stray wisps of sandy hair on top, and an ample belly testing the endurance of his custom-tailored suit. He smiled at Bolan, spoke in Dutch, then switched easily to English when he heard the reply.

"A safe-deposit box? Of course, sir. If you'd care to see Miss Dierken, right next door..."

"I'd rather have you help me," Bolan told him. "The fact is, I don't want to rent a box. I need to open one."

"In that case, if you have your key..."

"I don't. It's not my box."

The manager's smile was almost gone now. "I don't understand."

"Let's clear it up, then. Willem Ruud. Box 3172," Bolan explained, using the information Anika had given him. "I'm here to clean it out."

"It can't be done."

"You'll want to reconsider that," Bolan said, drawing back the left side of his jacket for a quick peek at the Walther automatic in its shoulder rig. "I know about the master key you keep for personal emergencies. There's nothing worth your life inside that box."

"You realize that this is robbery?"

"It crossed my mind. Now, shall we go?"

Bolan had considered looting Ruud's account, then dismissed the thought. A standard robbery took money from the tellers' drawers and left the vault alone. In any case, assuming he could pull it off, he'd be robbing customers he never heard of, more than likely leaving Ruud's account untouched—and heavily insured against the possibility of theft. A safe-deposit box, by contrast, would contain the precious secrets of its renter.

The manager looked vaguely ill as he led Bolan from his office toward the vault, but he made no attempt to warn the clerks or call for help. He clearly valued life more than the contents of a patron's safe-deposit box, and he had no good reason to believe the Executioner was bluffing. Bolan had the gun, the manager was scared enough to play along, and that was how he meant the outing to proceed.

The vault was cool and dry inside, with air-conditioning that whispered softly in the background. Bolan watched the manager consult a card file, then turn and lead the way between two rows of safe-deposit boxes that reached from the floor to forehead level, the larger boxes situated in the bottom rows. Ruud's box was in the lower left-hand corner, back against the wall. The manager was forced to kneel as he employed two passkeys, opened up the metal door and pulled the long box out.

"We have a booth—"

"I won't be needing it," Bolan replied. Opening the box, he scanned its contents: three compact computer disks, a ledger and a manila envelope that contained photographs.

He took it all.

"I know you have to call the cops," he told the manager when they were standing in the lobby, "and there's nothing I can do to stop you, short of staying here all day. But I've got men across the street, with automatic rifles. They'll be watching for the next six minutes, and they're being paid to drop the first man in a uniform they see. I hope we understand each other."

"Yes, of course."

"Don't feel too bad about Herr Ruud. This time tomorrow, you'll be wishing he was someone else's customer."

Five minutes later and two miles away, Bolan parked the car behind a service station and reviewed his booty from the bank. The small computer disks were perfectly inscrutable, but Bolan smiled while thumbing through the ledger. There were names, dates, figures—payoffs to at least three hundred persons, two of them with names he recognized from news reports. A judge and a legislator.

And the photographs.

He didn't recognize the faces, but he understood the game. Sex photos, snapped with hidden cameras, maybe lifted off videocassettes. It didn't take much thought to recognize the oldest blackmail scam of all. The targets would be politicians, influential businessmen, a fair cross section of the world where Willem Ruud was spreading out his tentacles, extracting tribute from the hapless idiots who fell within his grasp.

Bolan's next stop was the post office, where he placed his loot in a manila envelope, addressed to Freedom's Flower, in care of Anika Doorn. She'd find some use for the material when the smoke cleared. Bolan trusted her to flay the guilty and preserve the innocent.

Meanwhile, the Executioner had work to do.

THE WORST PART OF HIS JOB, Henrick Korstiaan thought, was how it dulled his appetite for sex. You couldn't hang around with naked people all day long, five days a week, and watch them coupling constantly, without becoming jaded. That hadn't been the case in the early days, of course. But now, fourteen months down the road, he was bored.

He'd been hired by Jani van Zon to stand watch while pornographic films were made and processed in a spacious loft on Gafflestraat in Rotterdam. He wore a pistol underneath his jacket, just in case, but so far there'd been no interference with the operation.

When he was still fresh on the job, he used to drift from one set to another, watching from the sidelines while a battery of actors, cameramen and directors cranked out three or four films simultaneously. In the lab, technicians processed film and printed copies by the crateload for distribution to adult theaters around the world. Each scene was also shot on videocassette, for a direct release to retail outlets and mail-order sales.

Korstiaan checked his watch, relieved to find that it was almost time for him to walk around the block and look out for anyone resembling spies from the church and civic groups that were forever trying to reform society by keeping sex behind closed doors.

He moved along a narrow hallway toward the exit that would take him down a dingy flight of stairs. His hand was rising toward the dead bolt when a powerful explosion punched the door right off its hinges, slamming into Korstiaan like a speeding truck and pinning him against the nearest wall. He was engulfed in smoke and cordite fumes, only half-conscious from the impact. Then the door fell over backward and he sprawled across it, like a stranded sailor on a raft.

He barely registered the stranger passing by: black shoes, dark slacks and a determined stride. He tried to raise his head, ask what was happening, but a part of his fuzzy brain already knew.

It was a bomb of some kind, and the man who'd set it off was past him now, proceeding toward the studio proper. Korstiaan wriggled on his pallet but found he didn't have the strength to rise.

There was a sound like canvas ripping, then screams and curses from the studio. Something collided with the wall behind him, hard enough to crack the plaster, and then there was a rush of bodies toward the exit, several of the runners stumbling over Korstiaan as they fled the smoky loft.

It could have been ten seconds or ten minutes when the stranger finally returned, bent down and rolled Korstiaan onto his back. The Uzi, with its bulky silencer, looked like a piece of field artillery, the muzzle inches from his face.

"You're still alive," the stranger said.

"I think so," Korstiaan replied.

"You have another job to do," the stranger went on.

"A job?"

It suddenly occurred to Korstiaan that they were speaking English. This was not a Dutchman, then. Somehow he thought the point might be important if he lived to make it known.

"I need a messenger, you need a break."

"A messenger?" Korstiaan echoed stupidly.

"I need a message taken to your boss. If you can do that, you have value to me. Otherwise..."

A jerky little motion with the Uzi said it all.

"What is the message?"

"This—he's going out of business. If he wants to cut his losses, he can give himself up to the police before I get to Amsterdam. Beyond that, he's as good as dead. Repeat it."

Korstiaan did all right, considering. The man seemed satisfied.

"You've got a fire back there," the stranger said. "It's spreading. Can you walk?"

"I don't know," Korstiaan told him honestly.

The stranger grabbed him by his collar and dragged him outside as if he weighed no more than ten or fifteen pounds. A few feet from the stairway, he was suddenly released. His skull cracked painfully against the floor.

"I'm leaving now," the tall man said. "If you've got any sense, you'll do the same."

Korstiaan had a choice to make. He could remain where he was and burn to death, or he could find the energy to run and the guts to face Jani van Zon with a message that could get him killed.

Not much choice at all.

THE HAGUE IS HALF AN HOUR from Rotterdam, an hour south of Amsterdam, but it is centuries away from either in appearance and demeanor. Named for a hedge, or *haag,* the city started as a tiny hamlet where Dutch royalty had their favorite hunting lodge. Today, while Amsterdam is technically the capital of Holland, the Dutch government is seated in The Hague, with three royal palaces, sixty-four foreign embassies and countless European headquarters for international oil, engineering and chemical firms.

Wherever tourists, businessmen and politicians flock together, there are also prostitutes. Bolan had no quarrel with sex between consenting adults, and he seldom gave a passing thought to prostitution, aside from its role as a staple trade item of organized crime. In Holland there were pimps and madams who obeyed the laws and paid their women fairly well. Some others, though, like Willem Ruud, grew fat and arrogant by flouting every precept of the law and common decency.

Their fortune lay in suffering, and it was payback time.

In the office block on Molenstraat, a team of lawyers occupied the ground floor, with accountants and a dentist on the second. Up on three, a child psychologist worked side by side with oil executives and publishers of college-level textbooks.

Bolan pushed a button for the elevator, then stepped into the car with six or seven other passengers when it arrived. Another button fixed his destination as the fourth floor, one below the penthouse suite of offices where high-priced architects dreamed cities up from scratch.

On four he left the elevator and sought his target at the far end of the hall.

Officially Molensky Enterprises was an advertising firm, with a small but lucrative sideline in public relations. Scratch the surface, though, and you'd find a group of lobbyists, spin doctors, payoff artists and extortionists controlled by Willem Ruud. Between Anika Doorn's report and information he had gleaned from Interpol, Bolan knew the company bought votes, bribed cops and judges, and fixed a jury now and then. It all worked out to Ruud's advantage—in the legislature, in the courts, in certain embassies and on the street.

The men behind that office door were sharks in human form, though Bolan doubted whether any of them had ever raised a hand in anger. They'd be far too civilized for that, aware that money carried more weight than a blackjack in the government and in the business world.

A receptionist smiled at Bolan from behind her antique desk—until she got her first glimpse of the Uzi.

Bolan nodded toward the door, and she was gone before he had a chance to appreciate her figure in the clinging knit dress.

He kept his mind on business as he moved down a corridor with private offices on either side. The first door opened at his touch, and Bolan saw a man in his forties talking on the telephone. A 3-round burst destroyed the small recorder that was taping both sides of the call and sent the pitchman sprawling, unhurt, backward over his swivel chair.

After passing an empty room, Bolan found two more men in the next office. One sat behind the desk, while his colleague stood, pointing to some information on a computer printout. Bolan let them see the Uzi, then cut the stander's legs from under him with parabellum rounds. He left the other crouched behind his desk, pleading for mercy.

Office number four was empty, and he doubled back to number three. He reached behind the desk and dragged the pale survivor into view.

"I'm betting you speak English."

"Yes."

"I have a message for your boss. You want to live, or should I give it to your friend down the hall?"

"No, I want to live," he whimpered.

"Tell Ruud he's running out of time. He can surrender, make a full confession, or I'll take him out. Can you remember that?"

"I can."

"Then you've got a call to make."

As Bolan spoke, he palmed the nearby telephone receiver and tossed it lightly toward the weeping figure. Instead of grabbing it, the man just closed his eyes and let it hit him in the face.

"I'd hate to think you'll let me down," Bolan said dispassionately.

"No, I promise you!" Already he was reaching for the phone.

The Executioner backtracked out of there, concerned that the receptionist could have police squads on the way by now. The elevator seemed to take forever going down, but he felt better when he hit the sidewalk.

Ruud wouldn't give up, of course. It would go against his nature. Bolan knew that when he'd left the messages, and that was fine. This way, when Ruud went down he'd know exactly what was happening and why.

By dusk, Anika Doorn felt as if the hotel room was closing in on her. Her problem, though, was that she had no place else to go. No safe place, anyway, while Willem Ruud's hired thugs were looking for her. If she just stayed where she was and waited out the night, perhaps even another day, Belasko would be finished with his work, and she could show her face again without fear.

It was no mystery why Ruud had chosen her, of all the Freedom's Flower members, for his first assault. She had been very active within the movement during the past two years, and she was often seen on television when a demonstration or petition made the news.

She thought about the tall American while she was in the shower, trying to rinse the feeling of fatigue and the smell of fear from her body. Belasko was a total stranger; worse, he was a man of violence who killed without remorse. The very fact of his existence indicated there was something seriously wrong with so-called civilized society. He was a hired assassin, nothing more. And yet...

Doorn was bemused by her reaction to this man she barely knew. It was a tired cliché: the damsel in distress who couldn't resist Prince Charming when he rescued her from danger. She rewarded him with a kiss, and they rode off into the sunset, to live happily ever after.

Toweling off, Doorn smiled at the idea. Belasko didn't strike her as the kind of man who settled down. They came from different worlds, quite literally. All they had in common was a shootout at the railway station and a short drive from the scene to her present hiding place. It hardly qualified as a romance, but she allowed herself the fantasy, aware that it could never translate into fact.

Her call to Mina Carstens had been reassuring, to a point. She'd learned that no one else from Freedom's Flower had been targeted, and while that pleased her, it was also disconcerting. If Ruud's syndicate was seeking her alone, it meant that all his resources would be committed to the task.

She'd used a false name when she'd registered at the hotel, and no one but Mina and the American knew where she was. It would have been more sensible to get away from Utrecht, but she'd drawn the line at that. The animals had chased her from her apartment, but she'd be damned if they'd make her flee the city.

She finished drying off and took the newly purchased terry robe from a hook behind the bathroom door. The fabric felt a little rough, but not unpleasant, on her naked body as she tied the belt around her waist. She spent another moment at the mirror, combing back her hair so that it lay flat against her head.

She leaned toward the mirror, both hands resting on the cool edge of the sink, and stared into her own reflected eyes. It felt as if they should look different, somehow—colder, with some visible suggestion of the spite that motivated her to wish Ruud and his soldiers dead.

She knew the reputation of such men. They never quit, spared no expense or energy until they bagged their man—or woman. It was the kiss of death to stand in opposition. Once they decided to eliminate a target, there was nothing to be done.

Enough!

Doorn had survived their first attack, albeit with the help of Mike Belasko, and there was no reason to suppose that they could track her down. When the smoke cleared and her enemies were dead, it would be safe to show herself again.

She switched off the bathroom light, humming to herself as she moved into the bedroom—and froze when she found three men standing there watching her. She didn't recognize their faces, but Doorn knew exactly who they were. Policemen would have knocked, and the hotel wouldn't have sent three men with guns to ask if she had ample towels.

THE HARD PART for Jani van Zon had been choosing which friend of his quarry's to squeeze. The group called Freedom's Flower boasted several hundred members who were known by name, an estimated thirty-nine of those in Utrecht, but he knew Anika Doorn's whereabouts wouldn't be common knowledge in the group. He had to find a special friend, and even that might not be adequate. There was no reason to believe Doorn would risk her life by reaching out to her familiar contacts, but he had to take the chance. And it was the only method van Zon could devise that held some prospect of results. A canvas of hotels would take forever, and she could be using a different name or using a disguise.

The plan was relatively simple, once he thought it out. He chose a member of the Flower club at random, Arabella van der Kopp, and dropped in for a visit at her home. If necessary, van Zon was prepared to work his way through the membership, but he got lucky on the first attempt. He had only two questions: Did the woman know Anika Doorn, and could she say if Doorn had any special friends?

The answers, after some persuasion, had been "yes" on both counts. Doorn's best friend within the group was Mina Carstens, also a resident of Utrecht. She was listed in the telephone directory, and that was all he needed.

Cleaning up, they'd arranged an accident for Arabella van der Kopp. How careless of her, balancing a radio beside the bathtub, where a simple nudge could drop it in the water.

Van Zon's second stop was Mina Carsten's apartment. He found her cooking supper. She resisted the questioning at first, until one of his soldiers held her face an inch or so from the electric burner on her stovetop. It was amazing how a touch of heat could loosen up reluctant tongues. Anika *had* called from a hotel, now that Mina thought about it.

A second "accident" was stretching things, but van Zon had no choice. One of his soldiers snapped the woman's neck, then positioned her so that a casual observer would believe she'd slipped and fallen in the bathtub. They let the shower run awhile, to leave her wet enough, and then they left.

Just one visit remained before van Zon could report to Ruud that the job was done.

The old hotel had little in the way of security. They went in through a service entrance at the back and made their way upstairs, looking for the room number Mina had given them. Without a passkey they were forced to pick the lock, one of the men working on it while the other stood beside him, a hand on his gun, prepared to kick the door and rush the woman if she started to scream.

Luck was with them, though. The door was barely cracked when van Zon heard the shower running. They'd wait and take her by surprise.

She looked quite fetching when she came out of the bathroom in her robe, her damp hair combed back from an angelic face. She gasped at the sight of van Zon and his men, stepped back a pace and raised one hand to clutch the robe shut at her throat.

"Who are you?" she demanded. "What's this all about?"

"We need to have a word with you, Miss Doorn."

"And that's why you break into my room?"

"It's urgent," van Zon told her, smiling.

"You could call me on the telephone," she answered.

"There's no time. I must insist you come with us."

"On whose authority?" Doorn tried to sound defiant.

Van Zon kept the smile in place and nodded to his soldiers, standing by with pistols drawn. "These friends are my authority. You will agree their argument is quite persuasive."

"I'm not going anywhere," she told him, her voice beginning to quaver.

"That would be a critical mistake."

"If you intend to kill me, you can do it here."

"Indeed I could... if that was what I wanted."

Van Zon was lying, but he didn't want to do his business here, with other hotel guests on either side of them and across the hall, only thin walls separating them. Anyway, Ruud wanted them to question her to see if she knew anything about their recent troubles, and a corpse couldn't respond.

She appeared to reconsider for a moment, then finally said, "I can't go out like this."

"Of course not."

"Will you leave me while I dress?"

"That won't be possible, Miss Doorn. We're all adults here."

Her cheeks were flaming as she turned away and moved toward the bed where she'd laid her clothing out. She tried to keep her back turned as she dropped the robe and reached for her underwear, but van Zon felt himself admiring her body.

Doorn had her dress on, and she turned to face him with a tough, defiant air. Van Zon admired the woman's courage, not that it would do her any good.

"Where are you taking me?" she asked.

"Someplace where we can talk without a lot of interruptions," van Zon replied. "We need a little privacy."

"I want them kept away from me." She glared at his men.

"I reward cooperation," van Zon told her. "On the other hand, if you should make things difficult, I cannot be responsible."

"Let's get it done, then."

She moved toward the door, almost before they were prepared. One of the men was there ahead of her, with a hand on the knob.

When Doorn made her move, it came with speed and grace, almost as if she'd rehearsed it. Wheeling in midstride, she drove one knee into the man's crotch and dropped him to his knees, a strangled gasp escaping from his lips. Before the others could react, she flung the door back, dodged outside and raced along the hallway, shouting for help.

Behind her, van Zon hit the hallway running, groping for the pistol in his belt. He had it drawn when his other soldier passed him, sprinting like a track star. He overtook Doorn near the stairs and slammed a fist between her shoulder blades.

She went down, sprawling. Before she could recover, yet another gunman grabbed a handful of her hair and hauled her upright, his pistol jammed beneath her chin. She struggled briefly but couldn't break away, and so she finally relented.

Van Zon scanned the hallway, waiting for a door to open, someone to emerge and challenge them, but no one came.

It was a long walk down the service stairs and out of the hotel.

God help us, van Zon thought. The job was turning into a nightmare. And when he considered Ruud's anger, the reward he could expect for yet another failure...

But they had the woman now, and she'd talk before he killed her. There was no way she could physically resist them, once he put his mind to work on making her confess. The rub would come, he realized, if she knew nothing after all.

Van Zon put the prospect out of his mind. He had come this far, and there could be no turning back. He knew exactly what he had to do, and he'd find out everything the woman knew about their enemy, no matter if it killed her.

Which, in fact, wasn't such a bad idea.

MACK BOLAN STOPPED a few miles south of Amsterdam and used the phone booth at a roadside gas station. On a whim he'd decided he should check in with Anika Doorn to find out if she had thought of any further information that would help him on the final lap of his campaign against the slavers.

And, he grudgingly admitted to himself, it would be good to hear her voice again.

The thought intrigued him, though he knew it would be going nowhere. They were as different as any man and woman could be. She had come to activism relatively late and pledged herself to lawful protest for the most part, until she found her back against the wall. In Bolan's case he'd been trained and retrained since his teens to be a warrior, blooded on the Asian killing grounds, committed to the notion that a savage predator responded to force, and force alone.

Aside from all their differences, the time and circumstances of their meeting also made the notion of a personal relationship absurd. Such a liaison would cost him precious time and energy, allowing his enemies to regroup and fortify their last line of defense.

Still, Bolan thought, it couldn't hurt to call.

He had the number for the hotel only, since she didn't know which room she'd be staying in when Bolan dropped her off. He got a desk clerk on the line and asked for Betje van der Klei, the name Anika was supposed to use on signing in. He waited while the clerk rang through, then the voice came back on the line.

"The lady doesn't answer, sir. If you would care to leave a message—"

Bolan's mind was racing, while his stomach tied itself in knots. Anika had agreed to stay in hiding until the smoke cleared, live on room service if necessary and to keep herself out of the public eye.

"You'd better check her room," Bolan said.

"We do not disturb our guests without good reason, sir. Miss van der Klei wishes privacy—"

"It's an emergency," Bolan replied, thinking fast. "She's a diabetic, and I know she wasn't feeling well when she arrived at the hotel. If you refuse to check on her, my next call goes directly to the fire and rescue team, my second to the press."

It did the trick. He counted off five seconds, then the clerk's voice came back in his ear. "Of course, sir. If you'd care to—"

"I'll hang on," Bolan said tersely.

The line filled up with music as he went on hold. He tried to recognize the tune, tried everything to keep himself from running down a mental list of things that could have happened to Anika. None of them was pleasant, and they all kept coming back to Willem Ruud and his first attempt to snatch her from the Utrecht railway station.

Bolan had already fed the pay phone half a dozen times and he was beginning to run low on coins when someone punched a button, reconnecting him. The desk clerk said, "There's no one in the room, sir. Naturally we're not responsible for guests who leave without—"

To hell with courtesy. Bolan cradled the receiver, then picked it up again while his brain retrieved the name and number he'd gotten from Anika, with this sort of emergency in mind. He made another call to Utrecht, this one to the office occupied by Freedom's Flower. Two rings later and he was talking to a woman.

"I need to speak with Dirk Christoffles," Bolan said.

"He's in a meeting at the moment, I'm afraid."

"Interrupt him!" Bolan snapped. "It's life and death. I have important news of Willem Ruud."

"A moment, please."

There was no music this time, but he heard a breathless, insubstantial whisper on the line that told him he was back on hold. Moments later a second, cautious voice came on the line.

"Hello?"

"Christoffles?"

"Yes." The stranger sounded like a man who has received his share of nuisance calls, and then some.

"You don't know me. I got your name and number from Anika Doorn."

"And you are...?"

"Never mind." Bolan laid the problem out in simple terms, beginning with the firefight at the railway station, but leaving out Anika's role as the initiator of the war on Willem Ruud. "She isn't in her room," he told Christoffles, winding down. "I figure if she got in touch with anyone, it would be someone from your group."

"Hang on," Christoffles said. "I'll check."

After some background noise, the man got back to Bolan and said, "No one here has heard from her since yesterday."

"Is that unusual?" Bolan asked.

"Quite."

"Okay. I'll be in touch."

"But, what—"

He severed the connection and jogged back to his car. It could be nothing, but he didn't like the odds. There was no way to test his gut reaction, but the Executioner had learned to trust his instinct.

Somehow, someone from the other side had traced Anika Doorn. There was at least a fifty-fifty chance that she was already dead. On the other hand, if he assumed the worst and let it go, her blood would be on Bolan's hands.

He knew exactly what he had to do, the only chance that he'd have to get her back. If she was dead, the effort still wouldn't be wasted, since his enemies would suffer. And if she was still alive, by some chance, there was a possibility that he could help her out.

He'd be going on to Amsterdam as planned, but with an altered strategy in mind. Hellfire was coming, and a man who earned his daily bread from human slavery was about to feel the heat.

16

Doorn didn't know where they'd taken her. Emerging from the hotel service entrance, the man in charge of her abductors put her in the back seat of a Volvo, forced her onto the floor and sat above her, with his left foot pressing on her neck. She tried to shake it off and got a sharp blow to the rib cage for her trouble, pain exploding through her diaphragm and robbing her of breath.

They drove for what seemed like hours without her watch to go by, but was probably more like thirty minutes. Time enough to put them in the countryside, though. She didn't recognize the landscape when they dragged her from the car, nor the smallish house with no close neighbors and a flower garden gone to seed.

It pleased her to discover that the gunman she'd struck still seemed to be in pain. He limped a little, glaring at her with a fierce expression on his face. Doorn knew that he'd hurt her, given half a chance, and she supposed that he'd have the opportunity before much longer. When it came, at least she could take satisfaction from the fact that one of them was marked, and that she hadn't gone quietly.

For all the good it would do her, though. Doorn didn't believe the leader's promise that they would release her, safe and sound, if she cooperated. Any fool would know she could identify them and would run to the police the moment she was able. The Netherlands had no death penalty for kidnapping, but they'd surely go to prison if she lived.

The room was small and plain, with no furniture and no windows. Folding doors concealed an empty, shallow closet. If she was going to escape, it would have to be through the door, and that was locked from the outside. But that would still leave her inside the house with three armed men who wouldn't hesitate to kill her, now that they were free of witnesses.

Her mind flashed back to the hotel in Utrecht, the disturbance she'd caused. None of the other guests had rushed to help her, and it was impossible to know if anyone among them had alerted the police.

Then it struck her, with all the impact of a fist between the eyes. She'd been careful not to use her own name when she'd registered at the hotel. Suppose someone had called the front desk, and the police were summoned. Then, what? They'd set off searching for Betje van der Klei, a woman who didn't exist—no home address, no friends or coworkers. No one, ultimately, who could identify her and direct the search.

How long would it be before her friends at Freedom's Flower grew concerned and started calling her at home? Another day or so, perhaps, by which time she'd almost certainly be dead. Her captors were determined men, and Doorn had no illusions of her own ability to suffer pain in silence. Oh, she would resist them for a while, but in the end she knew that she'd tell them anything and everything they asked.

And when they ran out of questions, they'd kill her.

Suddenly she thought of Mike Belasko. *He* could help her, but that presupposed his knowing where she was, or even that she was in trouble.

How long had it been since she'd seen him? Three hours? Maybe four, by now? He'd be on the road somewhere—perhaps The Hague, or Amsterdam. Why should he stop to call her, when he still had bloody work to do? It was impossible that he'd have dealt with Willem Ruud this soon. The very fact of her kidnapping told Doorn that the slaver was alive. Why else would his lieutenants waste time trying to defend him?

No, she could forget about Belasko for the moment.

She made another survey of the room, searching for a potential weapon this time, and again she came up empty. Trusting in the lock, her abductors hadn't bound her hands or feet, but there was no way she could overpower three men all armed with guns. Perhaps, if one of them came in alone, and she could find an opening...

Doorn frowned and shook her head. Following her near escape at the hotel, the men would watch her like a hawk and keep their weapons close to hand.

As if in answer to her thoughts, she heard footsteps in the hall outside her door. A key scraped in the lock and the knob began to turn.

THE CLUB IN AMSTERDAM was owned by Willem Ruud through nominees who drew a handsome salary and paid his taxes for him, while he skimmed a neat fifteen percent from gross receipts. Aside from serving gourmet dinners to a stylish clientele, it also doubled as a base of operations for an out-call service. A thousand guilders bought the customer an hour with the kind of prostitute who could pass for high-rent fashion models. That was just for openers, of course. For anything beyond a handshake, they'd have to strike a bargain that would run to several thousand more.

The place was still closed when Bolan parked his car out back and went in through the kitchen, making no attempt to hide the Uzi in his hand. The staff was already in attendance, but at the sight of Bolan's SMG and a nod from him in the direction of the door, they left hastily without a backward glance.

Bolan moved on to the dining room and found more help setting up, arranging silverware and folding napkins. He chose a table they'd finished and fired a short burst from the hip, exploding plates and glasses. The busboys made no argument when Bolan waved them toward the nearest door.

That left the office, where—unless he missed his guess—the manager would be busy preparing for another evening's trade.

The office door was open when he got there, and he could hear the sounds of a calculator and someone muttering in Dutch. A large man sat behind the desk in his shirtsleeves, with his tie pulled down and his collar open.

The Executioner caught the manager's attention as he crossed the threshold, the man's gaze following the silenced Uzi. He froze, spit out an expletive and raised his hands.

"Do you speak English?" Bolan asked.

"Yes." There was a strange strangled expression on his face. "Don't shoot me, please. Take anything you want."

"It's not a robbery," Bolan replied. "I've got a message for your boss, Willem Ruud."

The man flinched, as if he'd been slapped across the face. He didn't answer for a moment, his eyes still focused on the SMG. Then he slumped back in his chair, resigned.

"What is the message?"

"I want the woman, alive and well."

"The woman?" The man looked confused.

"He'll know exactly who I mean. You tell him anything that happens to the woman, happens to him. You have his number, I presume?"

"Yes."

"So make the call. Consider it a life-insurance policy. You'd better use a pay phone, though," Bolan added.

The man frowned in confusion. "I don't understand."

"A pay phone, somewhere else. Did I forget to mention you're about to have a fire?"

He gave the manager a running start before he palmed the first of four incendiary sticks and dropped it on the floor beside the desk. It flashed before he reached the hallway leading to the bar and dining room, smoke wafting out to follow him along the corridor.

He tossed a second fire stick toward the liquor shelf behind the bar and fired a short burst at the center rank of bottles, spilling alcohol to feed the flames. The last two Bolan pitched toward different corners of the dining room, and he was done.

There was no doubt in Bolan's mind that Ruud would get his message. Whether it would be in time, or how he'd respond, was anybody's guess. The Executioner, for his part, had no time for guessing games.

He had a war to fight, and he was past the point of no return.

BERG VOGEL FOLLOWED orders, even when he didn't understand the reasoning behind them. Take his new assignment, for example: standing watch at the old loft where women were received before they were packed off to cribs in Amsterdam and other cities. Jani van Zon's call had made the job sound urgent, rousting Vogel out of his apartment with orders to collect three more men and bring whatever guns they had available.

If Vogel thought about it, it reminded him of five—no, six—years back, when the Moluccans tried to cut in on the trade and sparked a shooting war. It hadn't lasted long, once the troops were mobilized, but the interlopers made a spirited defense for three weeks. Some two dozen men were killed, including one of Vogel's best friends in the business, cut down in a drive-by shooting on his own front doorstep.

Violence of that sort was rare in Holland, where the homicide detectives were efficient and aggressive, but there was always someone who wanted more, a larger slice of the pie, and would do anything to get it. When that happened, and a bit of discipline was necessary, it was easier to make the body disappear than answer lots of questions from police.

But this was different. Vogel felt it in his bones. The kind of preparations Jani was demanding meant some all-out threat was imminent, and Vogel knew he had to be ready.

There were eleven women in the holding loft when Vogel and his backup team arrived. Their job was simply to prevent the women from escaping and to make sure that no one else came in to see them without van Zon's personal okay.

The women held no interest for Vogel. They were clean enough, but they had a beaten look about them. That came with the "seasoning," he knew; cosmetics and a little rest would fix them up. When they got used to working in the business, it would be all right.

Vogel headed for the bathroom, situated in a corner of the loft. He splashed water on his face and tried to make himself relax. He rolled his head from side to side, the bones cracking.

The explosion rocked him on his heels. He drew his pistol, rushed back into the loft and found it filled with smoke that billowed from the direction of the windows. Plaster dust dribbled from the ceiling overhead, and Vogel saw a fellow guard stretched out on the floor, facedown.

The firing started with a single shot from a handgun. Vogel saw the muzzle-flash wink on and off through the drifting smoke before some kind of automatic weapon answered. It had a silencer attached, but he could still make out the sharp staccato sounds, immediately followed by a cry of mortal pain.

And there went another one of his cohorts, unless he missed his guess.

He moved directly toward the sound, though every brain cell he possessed was screaming for him to turn and run, do anything he could to save himself. But Vogel knew the chances of survival for a coward would be worse than those of a determined man in battle.

He was looking for a target when the man in black stepped up behind him and chopped his gun hand with sufficient force to send his pistol flying. Vogel pivoted to face the danger when another blow connected with his jaw. The room turned upside down, and when his vision cleared a bit, he found he was lying on the floor.

"If you understand me, there's a chance for you to see the sun come up tomorrow," the stranger said in English.

"I understand."

"You're all alone," the man in black went on. "The women will be leaving soon, without you. There are two ways this can go."

"Two ways?"

"You play along, do me a little favor, and you walk. Hang tough, and you can say goodbye right now."

"What kind of favor?" Vogel asked thickly.

"Take a message to your boss."

"I will."

"A wise choice. He has the woman. I want her. If she's damaged, I intend to pay him back tenfold. You got that?"

"Yes, sir."

"Fair enough. I'm leaving with the women now. You count up to a thousand, take your time, then hit the bricks. I'll take it personally if you let me down. One chance, that's all."

And he was gone. Vogel started counting, but he only reached two hundred by the time he heard the fire trucks coming, their sirens screaming like a soul in torment.

He found his pistol, tucked it out of sight and ran downstairs toward the street.

HE HAD RUUD'S NUMBER, literally, and it would have been an easy thing to call the slaver at his home, but Bolan had another plan in mind. He found a working pimp in the area and struck up a conversation. They were halfway through negotiating price when Bolan produced the Walther, gave the man a pat down and conveyed him to the waiting car. The plan was simple, and he filled his hostage in as they drove south.

Bolan chose the phone booth on its geographic and logistic merits. It was mounted on the wall of a drugstore that was closed for repairs, and the light traffic on the street was already thinning as the afternoon wore on.

He parked and let the pimp out first, still covered by the P-1 automatic. Bolan marched him to the public telephone and handed him a coin. "Call Willem Ruud," he said.

"I can't just call—"

The Walter made a soft metallic sound as it was cocked. "Your life depends on it," Bolan remarked.

Without further argument, his captive dropped the coin and started to dial, waited for a ring, and then told someone on the other end, "I need to speak with Willem. It's important."

"Is he coming?" Bolan asked.

"I think so."

"Give me that." He took the handset, keeping the pimp from moving with a sharp jab from the Walther. "Stay."

He waited half a minute before a man came on the line.

"Who's calling, please?"

"You wouldn't recognize the name," Bolan said, "but you've seen my work."

"Ah. The elusive Mr. X."

"I'm not so hard to find. The fact is, I was thinking I should drop by your place soon and introduce myself."

"I welcome you with open arms."

"You have the woman," Bolan said, cutting to the chase. "I want her back."

"Your messages were conveyed to me. Unfortunately I'm not sure—"

"The heat stays on until you let her go," he growled, interrupting Ruud. "If she's been harmed in any way, you pay the tab."

"You'll find I don't respond to threats."

"Respond to this."

He motioned for the pimp to step in closer, then handed him the telephone.

"What should I say?"

"Just introduce yourself," he said.

"Herr Ruud? It's Barend Wevers speaking, sir. I'm sorry to—"

He never finished the apology. The Walther's muzzle was two inches from his leg when Bolan fired, with no silencer to muffle the report. The impact slammed the pimp against the telephone. He collapsed, with one thick shoulder wedged against the wall. The handset dangled down his back, and Bolan picked up.

"You'll be running out of front men in a little while," he told the slaver. "And then it's your turn. Think about it while you have a chance."

He dropped the telephone again, before Ruud could reply, and walked back to his car. A gunshot demanded attention, and he saw two men approaching the phone booth as he drove away. They weren't close enough to read Bolan's license plate, and he wished them well on their discovery.

The gloves were off from this point forward. Ruud would either set Anika free, or he wouldn't. In either case the game had gone too far for Bolan to back off. It had to be scorched earth, eradication of the slaver's syndicate, and he couldn't trust the police to do a job that had eluded them for years.

His list of targets had been whittled, but there were still a few to keep him occupied before he went for Willem Ruud. By that time Bolan hoped he'd have some idea of what had happened to Anika.

And God help those responsible if Bolan found he was too late.

17

The Walther WA-2000 was an ultramodern sniper's rifle, designed to anticipate and eliminate most of a professional manhunter's problems with long-distance killing. For starters the weapon was constructed in a "bullpup" design, with the box magazine and action set behind the pistol grip and trigger group. This style reduced the rifle's length to slightly less than three feet, overall. The 25.5-inch-barrel was a free-floater, clamped at the front and rear for more stability, fluted longitudinally for cooling and the reduction of vibrations. With the built-in bipod, it was as steady as a rock, and there was no problem picking out a distant target with the Schmidt & Bender scope, a 2.5 × 10-power zoom. The Walther was chambered in .300 Winchester Magnum, six rounds slotted into the detachable magazine, and its self-loading action eliminated the distraction of using a manual bolt.

All things considered, Bolan thought it was the ideal killing tool. Too delicate for jungle work, perhaps, but he wouldn't be climbing any trees in Amsterdam. In fact, the rooftop perch would do just fine.

Across the street and fronting one of the canals that seem as plentiful as streets in Amsterdam, another office block stood square and grim against the skyline. He could check out any window on the west face of the building, but he concentrated on a corner suite of offices on the third floor from the top.

The company was one of several run by Willem Ruud, and while the slaver didn't appear to be in his office at the moment, others were on hand to keep the empire running smoothly in his absence. Bolan didn't recognize the men, but he could spot their type without a telescopic sight to help him.

White-collar crime wasn't a euphemism at the upper levels of the syndicate, where savages aspired to nothing quite so much as the illusion of respectability. Bolan focused on the office to his left, the inner sanctum, where a stodgy-looking man with silver hair was holding forth behind a spacious desk, three others seated in a ring before him, listening and taking notes.

They didn't look like savages or parasites, but Bolan knew these men for what they were behind the public masks. How many lives had been irrevocably changed—some flushed away like so much garbage—by decisions made in offices like this, each day.

He couldn't take them all; no man could ever manage that. But he could make a start, right here, right now.

Bolan fixed the cross hairs of his scope on the man behind the desk. His finger curled around the Walther's trigger, taking up the slack. He took a deep breath, filled his lungs with air, and then released a measure of it. His pulse was audible, a throbbing in his ears as he made the squeeze.

The Walther lurched against his shoulder, cushioned somewhat by the recoil pad. Downrange, 220 grains of sudden death drilled through the office window, traveling at 2,500 feet per second, spending 3,000 foot-pounds of energy at the point of impact. There was no drop at a hundred yards, but you could never really calculate the deviation of a bullet's course when it met physical resistance on the line of flight.

He'd been aiming for the mobster's nose and settled for a hit below the jawline. It was all the same at that range, with the bullet shredding flesh and smashing bone. A splash of crimson, blurred with motion through the sniper scope, and he was looking at an empty space behind the desk.

It took a heartbeat for the other three to realize exactly what was happening. Before they could react, the Executioner had shifted slightly, found his second target and was squeezing off.

A younger man had turned in his seat to face the window when Bolan caught him with a bullet at the hairline. Momentum pitched him backward, to sprawl in his nearest colleague's lap.

He, in turn, was on the verge of screaming when the third shot drilled his throat, an easy in-and-out from left to right. It severed the carotid artery and left him gagging.

And that left one.

The guy was up and running for the exit, when the fourth and final bullet found its mark between his shoulder blades. The impact punched him forward, just in time to catch the knife edge of the door as it swung open to admit a startled secretary. She jumped back, screaming, to avoid the dead man's fall.

It took another moment, packing up the Walther in its metal toolbox, for the hike downstairs. His coveralls gave Bolan the appearance of a workman, and there was no one to observe him on the service stairs. He hit the street and walked back to his waiting vehicle. There'd be time enough to change his clothes when he'd put some ground between himself and the dead men.

The Executioner had another target waiting down the road.

"IS THERE A PROBLEM, Willem?"

The warning call had put van Zon's nerves on edge, but there was still enough curiosity to make him ask the question, even when he saw the look on Ruud's face.

"Indeed there is."

Ruud shouldered past his first lieutenant and waited for the door to close behind him. He had more soldiers waiting in the car outside, but they wouldn't be needed here. His word was law with Jani.

"I'll fix it," van Zon said. "Just tell me what it is."

"I need the woman."

Ruud had called ahead, instructing van Zon not to harm the woman any further. She had to be alive and reasonably well when he arrived to pick her up.

"Where are we going?" van Zon asked.

"Not we. I need someone to stay behind and manage things. Someone I trust."

It was the highest flattery Ruud could manage, never mind that it might be a death sentence for his second in command. Subordinates could always be replaced.

"Whatever you think best, sir."

"Where is she, Jani?"

"In the back."

Ruud snapped his fingers, and one of his soldiers went to fetch Anika Doorn.

"She's fit to travel?"

"More or less." Disinterest showed on van Zon's face. "She won't be running any marathons, but she'll survive."

"I hope so, Jani."

"We were right, then, to suspect her. She has a friend."

"So it would seem."

"I'll kill him for you, Willem."

"That would be a good thing, Jani. Do it soon."

The soldier returned with Doorn. Her face was bruised along the left side, but otherwise, she seemed all right. She showed strain around the eyes, but van Zon hadn't broken her. Not yet.

"Herr Ruud." Her voice was ripe with scorn.

"Miss Doorn. We meet at last."

"You've come to help these pigs, then? I suppose they can't do much without your guidance, after all."

Defiant to the last. Ruud admired her spirit, even as he hated her for all the grief she'd brought upon his head.

"Actually," he said, "I've come to help you."

"I prefer to take my chances with the animals," she answered.

Van Zon stiffened and clenched his fist, but made no other move.

"Unfortunately," Ruud went on, "you have no say in the matter. This is not democracy in action, as they say."

"What, then?"

"We're going for a sea cruise, you and I."

"You need an extra anchor, I suppose."

"Under the circumstances, your sense of humor does you credit," Ruud said. "I would love to stay and banter with you all night long, but we must soon be on our way. We're driving up to Enkhuizen. I have a yacht there. Can I trust you to behave, or must we bind you like an animal?"

"Trust me?" Doorn smiled mockingly at that. "Herr Ruud, how could I possibly resist so generous an offer?"

"Very well. The handcuffs, Jani."

She didn't resist as her hands were pinned behind her back and the cuffs fastened onto her wrists.

Ruud cast a parting glance at van Zon as he turned to leave. "Be careful," he advised. "Do what you must."

"I won't let you down," van Zon assured him.

"Of course not, Jani. I don't expect you to."

IT CAME to van Zon afterward, as they were driving back to Ruud's house in Amsterdam, that he was to be sacrificed. Ruud was always practical. With Jani as his stalking horse, he had a chance to draw the enemy from hiding, catch him in the open and destroy him.

And if it failed, Ruud would still be safe behind the lines, with a hostage standing by in the event he was able to negotiate a truce.

It galled van Zon, being written off that way without a second thought, but he wasn't finished yet. He had a few tricks up his sleeve, and he was a survivor.

Ruud wouldn't mind if van Zon used his house as field headquarters for the coming battle. He was in no position to object, right now, and that helped, too. But van Zon would have gone ahead in any case.

It made sense to him that the enemy would ultimately come for Ruud at his home. Never mind that Ruud had taken to the water with his hostage; those who sought to bring him down would have no way of knowing that. The phone call from their spokesman, which had prompted Ruud to evacuate the city, promised someone would be coming for him soon. Van Zon believed that threat and clung to it, because it was his only realistic hope of locating the man he meant to kill.

Eliminating Ruud's most impressive enemy in years would place him in an excellent position to demand large favors and rewards. How could his boss refuse him anything, when he was the savior of Ruud's life and empire?

Feeling confident, van Zon went to the bar in Ruud's study, poured himself a double whiskey in one of the crystal glasses reserved for special visitors and walked back to the big recliner that he knew was Ruud's favorite chair. It seemed to fit him like a glove. His mind transported to a day when he would run the syndicate himself, and not for someone else's benefit. How sweet that day would be.

And he could feel it coming, sooner than expected.

Ruud had been weak and indecisive through the present crisis, waiting too long to organize a sound defense. It had been van Zon's plan to grab the woman, and he might have had a real lead to their common enemy by now if Ruud hadn't taken her away. As always, Ruud was thinking of himself and no one else.

That was a failing in a leader. Men of power should—

The rattling sound of gunfire catapulted van Zon from his chair, whiskey spilling on his pants and onto the thick shag carpet. He ran first to the nearby window, twitched the curtain back and peered into the darkness of the grounds. No muzzle-flashes were visible from where he stood, which confirmed his first impression that the shots had come from somewhere around the other side of the house.

He drew his pistol, hoping he wouldn't be forced to use it. Van Zon had no qualms about disposing of a man—or several, if it came to that—but he knew well enough that when a general had to fight, it meant his men were mostly dead or incapacitated.

He had fifteen soldiers on the grounds, which ought to be enough. The other raids had been conducted by small groups—in fact some survivors spoke of only one man at the several shooting scenes. Descriptions varied slightly, possibly influenced by panic, but it seemed to have been the same man every time.

A powerful explosion rocked the house, and van Zon heard a smoke alarm start to blare in its wake. He thought about how Ruud would react, then told himself it didn't matter. Ruud's enemies were looking for the man in charge.

And they'd found him, van Zon told himself.

He left the book-lined study, turned down the corridor and followed the chaotic sounds of combat toward the battle front.

It was his hour to shine.

BOLAN'S ADVERSARIES HAD attempted a defense in depth, but they were spread too thin to really make it work. One sentry had been spotted every hundred yards or so on the perimeter, but creeping dusk and Ruud's fondness for shade trees gave Bolan all the cover he needed for scaling the wall. There was also a lack of sensors, cameras or even razor wire to pick him out or slow him.

The Executioner was in his blacksuit, with the Walther P-1 leathered underneath his left arm. His lead weapon for the raid had been the Steyr AUG, lightweight and lethal, chambered for the 5.56 mm tumbling round. A bandoleer across his chest held extra magazines and several high-explosive MECAR rife grenades.

The AUG wouldn't accept a silencer and fire grenades in one configuration, so he took his chances. Time was more important to him now than stealth. Once he was on the property, the best thing he could do was rapidly engage the enemy and start to thin out the herd.

He got his chance eighty seconds after scrambling across the eight-foot outer wall. Two gunmen were approaching from his left, and Bolan let them come. He had the Steyr set for 3-round bursts, the stock braced against his shoulder, one eye peering through the standard optic sight.

As one gunman raised his shotgun, Bolan nailed him, then pivoted to drop the other one with a second burst before he even had a chance to draw his piece.

Two down—and that was it for the advantage of surprise. Unless the other troops were deaf, they had to know there was a problem on the grounds, and they'd be converging on the sound of gunfire any moment now.

Which meant that it was time for Bolan to move.

He started running for the house and met a third gunner along the way. He dropped him with a short burst to the chest. The man went down kicking, but the only shot he fired was wasted on the darkling sky.

When he could see the house ahead, the Executioner slowed long enough to fit the Steyr's built-on launcher. He then knelt, aimed and fired.

His target was a second-story window, and he came within six inches of a perfect bull's eye. Bolan saw the long projectile strike its target, blossoming in smoke and flame. At once a shrill alarm started inside the house, as if to summon anyone who might have missed the gunfire and explosion.

On the open lawn, two gunmen were closing on his left, a third man on the right. He took the doubleheader first, nine rounds to drop them in a heap of tangled arms and legs. A bullet whistled past his face, as the third gunman started firing. Bolan hit the deck, lay prone and sighted with the AUG.

The man tried to swerve aside and run for cover, but he was too late. A burst of tumblers caught him in midstride and knocked him sprawling. He rolled onto his back to stare skyward while the light went out behind his eyes.

It was as dangerous to sit and think about the enemy as it was to go and face them down. Bolan took no chances, and he was up and running by the time his latest victim had settled on the turf.

Hard driving toward the house, he saw two shooters on the porch, two more unreeling a garden hose to try to fight the fire upstairs. Bolan concentrated on the front-door sentries. They were bound to spot him any second, swing their guns around and—

There!

The closer of the two called out a warning to his sidekick, at the same time bringing up an Uzi. Bolan had the better weapon, greater range and superior experience. He started firing from the hip, still running, using up the last rounds in his magazine to slam the sentry back against the rail.

His partner was reacting now, as were the two men with the hose. There was no time for Bolan to reload the AUG. Instead, he whipped the Walther P-1 from its armpit rig and shot the nearest gunners first. One man took a bullet in the throat and staggered backward, dropping to his knees as blood spilled from his mouth. The other forgot about the fire and bent to reach a submachine gun lying on the grass. His posture made the target obvious, and Bolan shot him in the cranium.

Still dodging, running, Bolan found the second porch man, framed him in the pistol sights and squeezed off two quick shots. One parabellum round drilled through his adversary's chest and he went down.

As Bolan reached the porch, he ditched the Steyr's empty magazine and snapped a fresh one into place. A swift kick opened up the door and gave him access to the house. He crossed the threshold in a crouch, dodged to the left, then saw two gunners coming down the stairs. Their first defensive rounds gouged divots in the wall behind him, several bullets flying out the door, and then the AUG was spitting back, its aim and impact deadly.

They fell together, one man cursing while the other made no sound at all. Bolan waited for them at the bottom of the staircase, finishing the second shooter with a round between the eyes.

At once another gun went off behind him, bullets stitching ragged holes across the wall and chipping slivers from the banister. Bolan hit the deck and wriggled toward the nearest piece of furniture in search of cover. With a grenade in hand, he fixed it to the launcher and scuttled forward, looking for his mark.

Two gunners were firing from a doorway on the far side of a sunken living room, one with an automatic weapon, the other a handgun. There was barely time or need to aim, the MECAR round exploding just above the open doorway, raining wood and plaster. Bolan rose and went in through the swirling dust cloud, found one of the enemy dead from shrapnel wounds and nailed the other with a short burst to the chest.

Turning back toward the stairs, he caught movement on the landing overhead and spun in that direction, bringing up his AUG. A glimpse was all it took. Bolan knew Ruud's lieutenant from photographs he'd reviewed at Stony Man Farm. Now the target stood before him in the flesh.

He fired low, squeezing off two bursts before van Zon had a chance to use his pistol. Bloodied, the man slumped forward, tried to catch the rail with one hand, but lost it. He teetered for a moment, then fell.

It was a fair drop, fifteen feet or so, and Bolan thought he had to have killed van Zon, until the man's dark eyes opened. He stood above the wounded mobster, half expecting more guns to arrive at any moment, but they seemed to be alone.

"I want the woman," Bolan barked. "Where is she? Quick!"

"She's not here," van Zon said weakly.

"You have one more chance."

The man coughed blood, and Bolan recognized that he was running out of time.

"He took her. Willem."

"Took her where?"

"Enkhuizen. North. He has a boat."

"How long ago?"

"Perhaps an hour."

Bolan knew he'd get nothing more from the dying man. He hit the doorstep running, watching out for any gunners he might have missed along the way. He was an hour late, but she was still alive. Had been alive. The boat was trouble, though. He'd have to work it out, but he could do that on the drive.

The Executioner headed north.

18

The hasty preparation was a problem, but Bolan got it done. He had to drive from Amsterdam to Enkhuizen, roughly fifty miles along a winding coastal highway, but his first stop was a public telephone. He punched out the exchange for Utrecht. Dirk Christoffles sounded anxious when he picked up on the other end.

It took a moment for the Executioner to lay out what he needed. There was no resistance from Christoffles, but he had to call around to see what he could do. Bolan grabbed for the receiver on the first ring when the callback came ten minutes later.

Christoffles had a friend, who had a friend. There was a boat available and waiting for him at Enkhuizen, with a Nicolaas van Dych. Christoffles also had a fair description of Ruud's yacht. He'd call ahead of Bolan and try to pull some strings to find out where the yacht was going.

The drive was torture, standing on the pedal all the way. Ruud had an hour's lead, which meant that he could be at sea by now, well on his way to who knew where. Would he unload Anika Doorn when he was clear of land? A hasty burial at sea, perhaps, to ditch the evidence of kidnapping?

Drive faster!

When he reached Enkhuizen, he had to slow and follow the directions he received from Christoffles, winding through a maze of narrow streets to reach the waterfront, then counting piers until he found the boat slip he was seeking.

Nicolaas van Dych was in his fifties, stocky, with a face like leather and a fringe of sandy hair protruding from beneath his sailor's cap. He welcomed Bolan with a handshake made of iron, his manner serious. He knew Christoffles well and sympathized with Freedom's Flower in its work against the flesh trade. More importantly, perhaps, he had a penchant for adventure and couldn't resist the prospect of a chase at sea.

"There is a woman, I am told. A prisoner?"

"That's right."

"What will you do if you can find them?" van Dych asked.

"Try to get her back," Bolan replied.

"And the others?"

"Stop them any way I can. The law won't touch them. Someone has to try."

"You have a weapon?"

"Several," Bolan told him, choosing honesty.

"It's good to be prepared." Van Dych smiled for the first time since they'd met. "I also have a rifle on the boat. We must be going now."

"About our destination..."

"That is taken care of," van Dych told him, waiting while Bolan fetched a heavy duffel from the rental car. "Apparently the yacht is making for Denmark. We might catch her yet."

Two hundred miles, Bolan thought, if they put in to the nearest port of call, and farther if they kept on up the Danish coast. It was a break that van Dych had been able to discover even a general destination, as yachts weren't required to file a travel plan, like private planes.

Two hundred miles of open water, through the Ijsselmeer, the Waldenzee, the North Sea. Bolan had no information whatsoever on the yacht's capabilities in terms of speed or cruising range. If he assumed an average speed of ten or fifteen knots, the trip would take Ruud anywhere from twelve to eighteen hours from Enkhuizen to the nearest stretch of Danish coast.

Van Dych's boat was a smallish fishing vessel, old and weathered. He picked up on Bolan's first reaction, chuckling to himself. "You think she's old and tired?"

"Well..."

"Looks deceive, my friend. She might surprise you."

Bolan hoped so, but the fact remained that van Dych's boat was the only game in town. He'd have gone with a canoe if it had been his only hope of overtaking Ruud and rescuing Anika.

At sea, the boat did, in fact, surprise him, making close to twenty knots. If they could hold that speed, and Ruud's yacht was the least bit slower, they should overtake him in an hour or two.

But would they be in time?

Bolan had a sudden mental image of Anika, weighted down with chains and sinking toward the ocean floor, eyes bulging, bubbles trailing out behind her as she sank. It took a force of will to clear the mental slate and focus on his goal.

Speed was one thing; picking out their quarry on the open sea was something else. The North Sea shipping lanes looked nice and tidy on a map, but you could lose a tanker out there if it deviated in the slightest from a narrowly restricted course. It was a galling thought that they could miss the yacht altogether, and so lose the last, best hope of bringing Ruud to book.

But once again, van Dych surprised him.

"Radar," the Dutchman said, smiling as he registered his passenger's reaction. "An extravagance, some tell me. I use it fishing, sometimes. If Herr Ruud is out here, we will find him."

Bolan didn't share the sailor's confidence, but he went back to the afterdeck and started to unpack his duffel. He reloaded his weapons, checked extra magazines and arranged his grenades where he could reach them easily. He didn't know how many crewmen Ruud employed, or whether all of them were armed, but he assumed the two of them would be outnumbered three or four to one, at least.

When he was finished, there was nothing else for him to do but settle back and wait. The rest was up to Nicolaas van Dych and Fate.

IN FACT, Ruud's yacht had been held up at the dock for fueling, a delay of half an hour that infuriated the man and had him snapping at his crew. Doorn heard him storming up and down the deck above her cabin, and it struck her that he had to be nervous for a reason. It made no sense, after all this time, to think that he was frightened of a brush with the police. It had to be something else.

Belasko?

She could only hope, but even if he was pursuing Ruud, how could he find them now? Doorn didn't know where they were going when the yacht set out to sea, and she couldn't believe that Ruud had shared their destination widely.

Was it hopeless? Or did the American have skills that she was unaware of when it came to tracking down his targets?

Doorn knew she'd be ill before they even left the dock. She always felt mildly seasick on boats, and so avoided them whenever possible. Pills didn't help, and the feeling was sufficiently unpleasant that it spoiled the few seagoing trips she had attempted.

This one hardly counted. Doorn had a premonition that her journey would be interrupted somewhere in the middle of the ocean, when they came to drag her out and toss her overboard. She had no hostage value once they got away from Holland, and would become a major liability for Willem Ruud if she remained on board. Kidnapping was a serious offense, and while Ruud might be able to finesse the charges at home, Doorn was prepared to bet her life that his influence had its limits. He could run only so far, with hostages in tow, before he had to dump the excess baggage and move on.

Her cabin had no windows, so she couldn't tell the direction they were going. North along the coast meant Germany, then Denmark, possibly Norway or Sweden. South was Belgium, maybe France. Due west, England offered a potential sanctuary.

She gave up on the guessing game and tried to calm herself, employing all the tricks she knew. Deep breathing. Silent chants.

Nothing seemed to work.

She wasn't terrified of death, per se, so much as the ungodly forms it might assume when Ruud prepared to dump her. Would he use her first, or give her to his men? Would she be alive and conscious when they dropped her in the sea? Was drowning *really* the euphoric, painless fate described in fiction? What about the sharks and other creatures of the deep?

She tried to make her mind a blank, but her thoughts kept returning to Mike Belasko. Would he find her? Was he even looking for her? Did she have a chance of pulling through this mess alive?

One thing Doorn knew for certain was that when they came to get her, she would definitely fight. Despite her bound hands, she still had her teeth and feet. She'd resist with all her might, force them to kill her on the spot, instead of waiting for a slow and painful death.

Somehow, the notion seemed to put her mind at ease. Once death became inevitable, there was nothing left to fear.

She sat down on the narrow bunk and waited for her killers to arrive.

THEY SAW RUDD'S YACHT for the first time on the radar screen at half-past five o'clock. Van Dych made a correction to their course and goosed the throttle. Bolan was surprised to feel the boat shudder, picking up an extra knot or two of speed.

"I told you she'd surprise you," her captain said, grinning.

It would have been ungracious, also pointless, for Bolan to inquire if they had any realistic chance of catching Ruud. Van Dych would do his best, and guesswork was a waste of time that could be better spent in double-checking preparations for the firefight.

There was no doubt whatsoever that Ruud would mount a spirited defense. With that in mind the Executioner chose the Steyr AUG and MECAR rifle grenades as his lead weapon for the strike. The Uzi and the P-1 automatic both had shorter range, but the boat's pitch and roll would make the Walther WA-2000 virtually useless. The grenades gave him an extra punch, if van Dych could put him close enough to use them. It was risky, for Anika, but her plight wouldn't be improved if Bolan let Ruud's vessel slip away from him unscathed.

He didn't think it would be possible to sink the yacht with only four grenades. A lucky bull's-eye on the fuel reserve could do the trick, but that would be the most extravagant of long shots. Similarly a solid hit below the waterline with a MECAR round would take a miracle.

If nothing else, Bolan thought, he could try to blast the pilothouse and set the yacht adrift, then attempt to board her and dispatch his opponents at close quarters.

Bolan checked out the radar screen while van Dych poured on the steam. The blip seemed closer, but it was a matter of degree—mere inches on the screen, but miles away on open water.

"We're doing well," van Dych told him with a reassuring smile. "I think we'll catch her soon."

There seemed to be no adequate response to that, and Bolan didn't answer. They could only watch and wait.

"THERE'S A BOAT BEHIND us," the pilot stated. "And it's gaining, sir."

Ruud walked to the aft part of the pilothouse and peered through the windows, checking their wake. "I don't see anything," he said.

"It's still too far," the pilot replied, "but they're coming."

Ruud stepped out and crossed the afterdeck. The day was overcast and cool, gray water merging with the sky at the horizon. Was that a dark speck on the water, in the distance? Could it be a boat? Was someone in pursuit, or merely sailing in the same direction?

He walked back to the pilothouse and stuck his head in through the door. "More speed!" he ordered the pilot.

"Sir, we're at maximum performance now."

"You said they're overtaking us."

"Yes, sir."

"Then open up the throttle!"

"There's no more speed, sir."

"Damn it!"

Ruud slammed the door and stalked back to the railing. The black speck on the water did, indeed, seem closer.

Thirty minutes later there was no denying it was a boat, perhaps one-third the yacht's length and many years her senior. Ruud used binoculars to check it out, but saw nothing to suggest the boat was a police launch or a military vessel. He focused on the small boat's wheelhouse. He could see only two men in there, one taller than the other by at least six inches, their features unidentifiable through the murk and dirty windows of the smaller boat. For all he knew, though, there could be others crouching below his line of sight, or waiting in the space belowdecks for the signal to attack.

When the tall man left the wheelhouse and moved to stand at the rail, Ruud got a better view of him and the rifle slung across his shoulder.

Ruud retreated from the stern rail and called for his on-board troops. Eight men responded instantly, all bearing arms, which still left three to operate the yacht. Snapping orders, Ruud positioned his men around the deck where they had cover, interlocking fields of fire.

That done, he stalked back to the pilothouse. "How long before they overtake us?" he demanded.

"Twenty minutes," the pilot said. "Maybe half an hour."

"When they approach us, you must follow my instructions absolutely. Is that understood?" Ruud barked.

"Yes, sir."

Ruud knew he had to find out whether Anika Doorn knew who was pursuing them and how far they'd go to win her freedom.

All the way, perhaps.

If so, Ruud meant to see them dead.

BOLAN SCANNED THE YACHT through the binoculars van Dych had loaned him. He saw the gunners fanning out, taking up their positions. Ruud's men were packing automatic weapons, two of them with AK-47s, while the others carried submachine guns, all with shorter range. The riflemen would be his first priority.

He walked back into the wheelhouse. "They're expecting us," he said to van Dych.

"I see them." If van Dych was frightened, he concealed it well. He reached down beside his chair to hoist a vintage Mauser rifle. "Let them do their worst."

"Okay. Let's do it."

Back on deck, Bolan drew the first grenade, fixed it to the Steyr's launcher and calculated the distance. The 40-mm grenade had an effective range of one hundred meters. They were almost close enough, but that would put him within range of the Kalashnikovs. The trick would be to knock them out of action the early moments of the fight, before they had a chance to bring him down.

He had the gunners spotted as their boat closed to firing range. The riflemen were separated, one to port on deck, the other stretched prone atop the cabin. Based on angles and the field of fire, he viewed the rooftop gunner as a greater threat and sighted on him first, his finger taking up the trigger slack.

Bolan was reaching for the second grenade when the two Kalashnikovs cut loose, but too late to save the gunner firing from the cabin roof. The high-explosive round went in on target, detonating with a smoky thunderclap. He glimpsed a rag-doll figure becoming airborne, and then the yacht seemed to veer off course a fraction as the shock wave reached her pilot.

Crouched on the deck, Ruud's second rifleman milked short bursts from his AK-47, peppering the boat's stem and foredeck, several bullets passing close enough for Bolan to hear them buzz by like angry hornets. The Executioner sighted on his muzzle-flash, then raised the Steyr's muzzle just enough to put his next round on the bulkhead, rather than aiming at the man himself and risking a shot overboard.

Bolan waited for the blast, a swirl of smoke and flame that cleared in seconds. The wounded gunner lurched toward the rail, his AK-47 trailing by its sling. Another 3-round burst, and the man was hurled across the rail and into the water.

That left half a dozen shooters Bolan knew about, with perhaps more hiding out in reserve belowdecks. Submachine guns began to rattle from the yacht, muzzle-flashes winking from the starboard railing, the companionway, the afterdeck and an open porthole.

Bolan mounted grenade number three and chose his mark. Logic told him Ruud would have Anika in a cabin, well belowdecks. He marked the gunner firing from the mouth of the companionway and let him have the next explosive round. A ball of fire erupted in the open hatch, windows erupting in a spray of fractured glass from the concussion.

Smoke was trailing from the yacht now, not just from the strike points of Bolan's high-explosive rounds but from a fire belowdecks. The vessel didn't seem to be in immediate danger of sinking, but Bolan knew what fire and smoke could do in a confined space, especially to captives. Soon, he'd have to make his move, instead of sniping from a distance.

Bolan primed his last grenade and braced his leading elbow on the rail as he leaned over, aiming for the stern of the yacht. He focused on the transom, just above the waterline, hoping to score a fair hit on the rudder and the screws.

He fired the round and watched a smoky geyser spout up from the stern. The yacht shuddered, veered to starboard, then stalled.

It was the best chance they'd have, and van Dych leaned on the throttle, swinging to the port side of the yacht, where one of Ruud's gunmen seemed to hold the fort alone. At forty meters, he began to take on human features, firing from the hip as he fell back in search of cover.

Bolan tracked him with the Steyr's optical sight and stitched a 4-round burst across his chest. The gunman staggered and went down.

Van Dych continued to swing toward the yacht. Bolan stood at the prow, his rifle clenched in one hand with the sling around his neck, his free hand on the rail. With six feet between the vessels and no one on the spot to challenge him, Bolan took the gap in a desperate leap.

He made it, and immediately started moving toward the metal stairs that would take him to the pilothouse. He was almost there when a gunman came around the corner, leading with his SMG and looking for a target. Bolan met him with a rising burst of 5.56 mm tumblers that propelled him backward, blood spouting from his chest.

He reached the stairs and started up them, then froze at the sound of an enraged voice behind him. He swiveled, dropped to a crouch and fired the AUG one-handed, homing on his mark by instinct.

The gunner was armed with an Uzi, but it didn't help him when a stream of armor-piercing bullets opened up his chest. Almost before he fell, the Executioner had ditched his magazine and snapped a fresh one into place behind the Steyr's pistol grip.

Bolan took the rest of the stairs at a sprint and barged into the pilothouse. The skipper gaped at him like a man who'd seen a ghost.

"Do you speak English?" Bolan asked.

The man gave a jerky nod, his vocal cords betrayed by fear.

"Okay, the choice is swim or die," Bolan said, punctuating the words with a choppy motion from the AUG. "Do you follow me?"

The man was clearly used to taking orders. He edged past the Executioner, descended to the deck and threw himself across the rail into the sea.

Another short burst from the Steyr knocked out the radio and navigation gear. The engine labored on, but the screws or the rudder had clearly been damaged. The vessel wouldn't be going anywhere without a tugboat to provide the power.

Bolan started down the stairs again and found two shooters waiting for him. One was halfway up, the other covering his blind side from the deck. They'd obviously been following the sounds of gunfire, yet they still seemed startled when their enemy appeared before them in the flesh.

They hesitated; Bolan didn't.

Firing from the hip, he took the nearer shooter first and blew him backward down the stairs.

The second gunner sidestepped quickly, barely noticing the death of his companion as he brought the submachine gun up and into target acquisition. Bolan knew this could be it, the moment he'd managed to evade for years on end, but he couldn't surrender to the feeling. He raised the AUG, his finger taking up the trigger slack, a fraction too late to make the cut.

His adversary suddenly seemed to stumble, then fall to his knees, losing the SMG. The reason came a heartbeat later, with the flat sound of a rifle shot from the direction of van Dych's boat. Glancing in that direction, Bolan saw van Dych lower his Mauser, then turn back to focus on the handling of his vessel.

Bolan stepped around the fallen body and headed in the direction of the doorway that would take him to the cabins down below—and met the final gunman there, soot-blackened, bleeding from a narrow gash along his hairline. In spite of his wound, he appeared more than capable of killing with the Ingram MAC-10 he carried. The stubby SMG had an advantage at close range, but Bolan didn't give him time to use it. He lunged forward with a buttstroke from the AUG that slammed the man against the nearest bulkhead, then finished it off with a round between the eyes at skin-touch range.

He moved on.

The smoke was clearing a bit belowdecks, and he passed a used fire extinguisher. Ahead of him, the corridor was lined with staterooms, three on either side. He was prepared to search them all, if necessary, when Ruud chose that moment to emerge from the second door on the left, Anika thrust before him.

Ruud held a shiny automatic pistol, the muzzle buried in Anika's golden hair. Her face was bruised, but she seemed to be holding on.

"That's far enough," Bolan ordered the slaver.

"I don't think so," Ruud replied. "The lady wants to live, you see. That won't be possible unless you let me go."

"Go where?" Bolan asked mockingly. "We're adrift here, and your pilot just went overboard. You're also short of guns, from where I stand."

"I only need the one," Ruud said. For emphasis he gave the shiny piece a twist that made Anika cry out in pain.

"And if you kill her, then what? Where's your shield?"

"Perhaps I should kill you instead."

"Try it," Bolan offered.

"A hero? I wasn't sure there were any left. Some friends in Copenhagen are expecting me. I'll have to take your boat. It's only fair."

"No dice," Bolan said shortly.

"I expected you to show more concern for Miss Doorn," Ruud responded.

"My concern includes preventing you from taking her."

"We have a standoff, then."

"Not quite."

The Executioner didn't waste time considering his shot. He knew the angles, had had his target marked as soon as Ruud had shoved Anika from the stateroom. All he had to do was raise the muzzle of his AUG a few more inches, brace the bullpup stock against his hip and squeeze.

The bullet struck Ruud's forehead, half an inch above one eye, and snapped his head back with the impact of a roundhouse punch.

Blood spattered Anika's face, and she nearly fell as Ruud slumped backward, lifeless fingers snagged inside the collar of her blouse. She struggled free, ran to Bolan and threw her arms around his neck.

He didn't have to check on Ruud. The slaver had received his final payoff from the misery of innocents.

Topside, they found a pair of crewmen standing at the starboard rail, their hands raised to the sky as van Dych covered them with his Mauser. He smiled like a hungry cat surrounded by canaries.

"Should I kill them?" he asked, preparing to fire.

"There's no need for that," Bolan replied. "They're not going anywhere."

"And us?" van Dych asked.

"We're going home."

EPILOGUE

"You're leaving soon," Anika said. It didn't sound like a question.

"I'm booked on the red-eye out of Schipol," Bolan told her, glancing at his watch. "But I've still got some time."

They occupied the corner booth of a small restaurant. Bolan's call to the authorities at Enkhuizen had been made anonymously from a public telephone, with no link to Nicolaas van Dych, Anika Doorn, or Freedom's Flower. If the two survivors from Ruud's yacht talked to the police beyond the bare essentials, it would be their word against a battery of locals standing by to give van Dych an iron-clad alibi.

"Where will you go from here?" Doorn asked.

"Back to the States. A little downtime, I suppose. And you?"

"There's still a lot of work to do in Holland. You've helped us greatly, but the struggle still goes on. Ruud wasn't the only slaver in our country, or in Europe, for that matter."

"I wish you luck," Bolan said.

"And the same to you. But somehow, I think you'll need it more than I will."

"You can never tell." Bolan hesitated. Then decided to risk it. "If you hit another snag, I guess you've got my number."

"More or less," Doorn answered, smiling.

"I get messages," he told her. "They're a little late sometimes, but they get through."

"I won't forget," she said, and Bolan understood that she wasn't referring strictly to the contact number.

"I won't either."

"I wish..." She hesitated, her eyes downcast, examining the contents of her coffee cup. When she glanced up again, her eyes were shining. "I just wish you didn't have to leave so soon."

Bolan was tempted. There was nothing urgent right now back in the United States. A break might do him good.

"What did you have in mind?" he asked.

A blush rose in the woman's cheeks. "You haven't had much chance to see my country," she replied. "Not as it should be seen. If you had the time to spare, I might... that is... we could...."

She floundered then. Bolan picked up the pause and went with it.

"I'd have to make some calls."

"Could you?" Her smile was radiant, and it warmed him inside.

Brognola might have questions, but he wouldn't press it.

The war could wait a few days.

He smiled back at Anika.

"So," he asked, "where's the telephone?"